THE DAY BEFORE FOREVER

and

THUNDERHEAD

By Keith Laumer

Non-fiction

HOW TO DESIGN AND BUILD FLYING MODELS

General Fiction

EMBASSY

Science Fiction

WORLDS OF THE IMPERIUM

ENVOY TO NEW WORLDS

A TRACE OF MEMORY

THE GREAT TIME MACHINE HOAX

A PLAGUE OF DEMONS

GALACTIC DIPLOMAT

THE OTHER SIDE OF TIME

THE TIME BENDER

RETIEF'S WAR

CATASTROPHE PLANET

EARTHBLOOD *(written with Rosel George Brown)*

THE MONITORS

NINE BY LAUMER

THE DAY BEFORE FOREVER *and* THUNDERHEAD

THE DAY
BEFORE FOREVER
and
THUNDERHEAD

by Keith Laumer

1968

DOUBLEDAY & COMPANY, INC., GARDEN CITY, NEW YORK

Contents

THE DAY
BEFORE FOREVER

PROLOGUE

Somewhere a bell was ringing. The Old Man reached out in the darkness, fumbled across rumpled silks for the heavy velvet pull cord. He tugged it twice, imperiously.

"Sir!" a voice responded instantly.

"Get him!"

The Old Man lay back among the scattered cushions.

He's alive, he thought. *Somewhere in the city, he's alive again. . . .*

CHAPTER ONE

It was a narrow street, without curbs or sidewalks, jammed between flat gray walls that ran in a straight line as far as I could see. Misty light filtered down from above on a heavy ornamental ironwork gate set in the wall across the way. There were no people in sight, no parked cars, no doorways, no windows. Just the wall and the gate and the street, and a rumble through my shoes like heavy machinery grinding up boulders in the distance.

I took a step away from the wall and the pain hit me. The top of my skull felt like the place John Henry had picked to drive his last spike. Cold rain was trickling down my face and a cut on my lip was leaking salty blood that mixed with the rain. I looked at the palms of my hands; they were crisscrossed with shallow cuts, and there was rust and grime in the cuts. That started me trying to remember when I'd had my last tetanus shot, but thinking just made my head hurt worse.

A few feet to the left an alley mouth cut back into the wall behind me; I had a feeling something unpleasant might come out of it any minute now, and a little curiosity stirred as to what might be at the other end, but it was just a passing thought. I needed a dark hole to crawl into and hide before I could take a lot of interest in unimportant matters like where I was and what I was running from. I got a good grip on my head and pushed away from the wall. The pavement rocked like a Channel steamer in a three-quarter gale, but it stayed under me. I made the thirty feet across the street and put a shoulder against the wall to steady it and waited for the little whirly lights to go away. My pulse was hammering a little, but no worse than you'd expect after the kind of weekend that could put a man out on a strange pavement talking to himself. The chills were fading out now, and I was starting to sweat. My coat felt tight under the arms, and the collar was rubbing the back of my neck. I looked at my sleeve. It was stiff, shiny cloth; no class, no style. Somebody else's coat. I breathed through my teeth a few times to blow some of the fog out of my brain, but it didn't seem to help. It must have been one hell of a party, but it was all gone now, like easy money.

I checked my pockets; except for some loose threads and a pinch of lint I was as clean as a Salvation Army lassie catching the last bus back from the track.

The placard attached to the gate caught my eye. Weathered block letters spelled out:

PARK CLOSED AT SUNDOWN
BY ORDER OF COMMISSION
ENTER AT RISK OF LIFE.

I looked through the gate. If it was a park, there might be a nice patch of grass to lie down on. The line about risk of life might have called for some looking into, but next to a nap, what was a little gamble like that? I pushed on the iron curlicues and the gate swung in.

2

White marble steps led down, flanked by big urns full of black fronds. At the bottom, a wide flagstone walk led away between clipped borders and flowering shrubs. The dark green smell of night-blooming flowers was strong here; I heard the soft play of water in a fountain that caught reflections from lights strung in the hedges. Away in the distance beyond the park other lights crossed the sky in rows like high bridges. The light breeze made lonesome noises in the branches over me. It was a nice place, but something in the air kept me from wanting to curl up on the grass and compose a sonnet about it.

The walkway I was on was of patterned brick, bordered by little white flowers that led away into the shadows of trees. I followed it, listening for sneaky footsteps behind me. As far as I could tell, there weren't any; but the exposed feeling up my back didn't go away.

There was something on the grass, under the trees ahead. Something pale, with a shape that I couldn't quite make out. At first I thought it was an old pair of pants; then it looked like a naked man lying with his upper half in shadow. I kept on trying to make it look that way until I was ten feet from it; at that range, I quit kidding myself. It was a man, all right; but his upper half wasn't in shadow. It wasn't there at all. He'd been cut in two just below the ribs.

I circled around him, maybe with a vague idea of finding the rest of him. Up closer, I could see he'd been bisected by hand, not neatly, but in a businesslike way, as if the cutter had a lot of carcasses to get out tonight and couldn't waste too much time on fancy cleaverwork. There wasn't much blood around; he'd been drained before being cut up. I was just getting ready to roll him over in case he was lying on a clue, when something made a little sound no louder than a grain of corn popping.

I moved off across turf like black Wilton, stepped in under an odor of juniper, and stared at a lot of shadowy shapes that might have been twenty-man gangs for all I knew, and waited for something that seemed to be about to happen. A minute went by that way.

With no more sound than a shadow makes moving on a wall, a man stepped into view fifteen feet from me. He put his head up and sniffed the air like a hound. When he turned his head his eyes caught the light with a dull shine. He stood with one shoulder high, the other twisted under the load of a hump like a crouched monkey. His face was pockmarked, and there were scars across his shaved skull. A lumpy strip of keloid ran from under his left ear down under the collar of a thick sweater. Heavy thigh muscles showed through tight pants with a camouflage pattern of diagonal gray lozenges. There was a heavy wooden handle in his belt with a blade that was honed to a thin finger of steel like a butcher's trimming knife. He swung slowly; when he was facing my way, he stopped. I stood still and tried to think like a plant. He squinted into the shadows, and then grinned, not a pretty grin.

"Come out nice, sweetie." He had a husky bass growl that went with the scar on his throat. "Keep the hands in sight."

I didn't move. He made a quick motion with his left hand; there was a soft sound and a second man came out of the bushes on his left, hefting a working length of iron pipe. This one was older, wider, with thick arms and bowed legs and a stubbly beard shot with gray. He had little sow's eyes that flicked past me and back.

The hunchback touched his filed blade with a finger and said, "All alone in the park, hey? That ain't smart, palsy."

"Chill the buzz," the one with the beard said through his left nostril. "Slice it and haul, that's the rax."

He reached inside his shirt, brought something out gripped in his fist; I got a whiff of a volatile polyester.

The hunchback moved closer.

"You got anybody'll buy you for live meat?" He talked with a lot of mouth movement that showed me a thick pink tongue and broken teeth. Off to my left, somebody was generating a fair amount of noise making yardage around to my rear. I ignored that, ignored the question.

"Better open up." The hunchback slid the knife out and held it on his palm. I took a step out from under the tree then.

"Don't scare me to death," I told him. "I've got friends on the force."

"Talks like a Cruster," the bearded one whined. "Caw, Rutch, take the mothering weed down and let's fade."

"Try me, baby," I threw a line at him, just to keep him interested. "I eat your kind for breakfast."

Behind me, a stick cracked. Rutch tossed the knife on his palm, then stepped in and feinted short. I didn't move. That meant I was slow. Beaver hefted his pipe and took a bite out of the inside of his cheek. Rutch was watching my hands. He didn't see any guns, so he moved in that last foot and gave the high sign.

Behind me, the Indian fighter took a noisy step and wrapped arms around me and leaned back. That put him where I wanted him. I used my right shoe to rake down his shin and tramp hard on his arch. The grip slipped an inch, which gave me room to snap-kick the hunchback below the knee. The bone went with a crunch like a dropped plate. I gripped hands with myself and gave the lad behind me a couple of elbows in the short ribs; he *oofed* and let go and Rutch fell past me in time for me to meet Beaver coming in with his club swung up overhead like the royal executioner getting set to lop off a head. I caught his arm between my crossed wrists, shifted grips, and broke his elbow. He hit on his face and squealed and the club bounced off my back.

The one who had done the back door work was on his hands and knees, coming up. He looked like a half-breed Chinaman, with a wide, shiny face and lots of unhealthy-looking fat along the jaw line. I sent him back with a knee to the chin and stood over him, breathing hard; my wind wasn't what it should have been. I was glad none of them looked like getting up.

The Chinaman and the beard were out cold, but the one called Rutch was humping on the grass like a baby mouse in a bonfire. I went over to him and flipped him on his back.

"Your boys are soft, and too slow for the work," I told him. I nodded at what was on the grass. "Yours?"

He spat in the direction of my left knee and missed.

"Nice town," I said. "What's the name of it?"

His mouth worked. The stubble on his head was orange-red, and up close I could see the pale freckles across the knob of gristle he used for a nose. A tough redhead, in spite of the crooked back. I put a foot on his hand and leaned on it.

"Tell it, Red. What's the racket?"

He made a move and I leaned a little harder.

"Deathers . . . in the park . . . tonight . . . !" He said it in quick gasps, like a drowning man dictating a will between waves.

"More detail, Red. I catch on slow."

"Blackies . . ." There was a little foam at the corners of his mouth and he was grunting softly, like a hound dreaming of rabbits. I didn't blame him for that. A broken knee is pretty hard to bottle up. Then his eyes rolled up. I started to turn away, half heard the sound and swung back, saw the shine on the blade in his hand an instant before the blow low on my back and the hot-poker pain of the knife going in.

3

The shock effect on the human nervous system of a stab wound varies a lot with different subjects. Sometimes the victim falls out flat on his face before he's lost the first ounce of blood. Other times he'll walk home, go to bed, and quietly bleed to death, unaware that he's even been hit. With me it was somewhere in between. I felt the blade hit bone and deflect upward, and all the while my right hand was coming around edge-on in a flat arc that connected with Red's superior maxillary just below the nose, a messy spot. He fell back hard and didn't move, and I stood over him, trying to get hold of my side with both hands. A heavy pulse was gushing down over my hip like a spillway. I took three steps, felt my knees going, sat down hard on the ground, still trying to hold the wound closed. I was clear-headed, but the strength had gone out of me. I sat there listening to my pulse hammer in my ears and thinking about trying it again just as soon as it quieted down.

Come on, Dravek, on your feet. Back home you're supposed to be a tough guy. . . .

I made what I thought was a move to get up and went over sideways, slowly, like an old tree falling. I lay there with a mouthful of sod, listening to the wind sighing in the trees, a soft gobbling sound from Rutch or one of his boys—and another sound, like stealthy feet creeping up through the underbrush. Or maybe it was just the bats flapping their wings in the attic. My eyes were wide open and I could see the fat Chinaman's feet, and beyond him a lot of black shadows. One of the shadows moved, and a man was standing there, looking at me.

He was small, lean, spidery, dressed in tight black. He came across toward me, through a sort of luminous mist that had sprung up suddenly. I thought of a couple of things I wanted to say, but somebody had cut the strings operating my talk-box. I watched him skirt the Chinaman, come over, and stop a couple of feet from me. It was very dark now; I could barely make out the shape of his boots against the black. I heard a sound that seemed to be a nice easy laugh, like a guy who's just heard a mildly funny joke, and a voice from a long way off seemed to say, "Neat, very neat. . . ."

Things got hazy then. I felt hands moving over me; the pain in my side was like a line of fading red fire.

"Lie still," somebody said in a whispery voice. "I have to stop the bleeding."

I started to say that Red had put the point in an inch too high, that all he'd sliced was fat and gristle, but it came out as a grunt.

"I gave you a shot of fun juice," the same voice said. It was a breathy tenor, as soft as a fog at sea. "It was all I had."

The hands did some more things that hurt, but it was a remoter pain now. A nice warm feeling was spreading up my side. I lay still and breathed.

"There," the voice said. "Do you suppose you could stand?"

I grunted on purpose this time and rolled over on my face. I got my knees under me and rested on all fours, watching the trees sail past like the view from a merry-go-round.

"We'd better hurry," the little man said. "They're close."

I said, "Yeah," and got my feet under me and climbed to my feet like a weekend Alpinist doing the last few yards to the top of Annapurna. We looked at each other across a stretch of smooth-mowed grass unmarred by anything except three and a half corpses. He was a slender-built, dainty-moving man with the sharp, complicated features of a Bourbon king, a sleek, narrow head with bugged-out eyes set on the corners of it, deft hands in black kid gloves. The tight pants were tucked into short boots, and he wore a ducky little vest with ruffles along the top edge over a black turtleneck.

"Who were they?" I asked, just to break the silence. My voice came out in a croak.

He glanced down at the nearest of them, who happened to be the Chinaman; the fat face had that vacant, collapsed look you see on photos of bodies found on a battlefield. The little man lifted a lip and showed me a row of sharp teeth that were too white to be real.

"Scum," he said delicately. "Baiters; cold-meat men. Their kind are the lowest of the low." He laughed. "Whereas I am the highest of the low." I could hardly hear him for the zinging noise in my head. My legs felt like something snipped out of cardboard. I rubbed the back of my head, but it didn't help. I still felt like a guy who's stepped into what he thought was the men's room and wound up in the third act of *Aïda*.

"You a cop?" I said.

"A . . . ?"

"Cop. Dick. The law."

He said "ah" and lifted his chin. A light came and went behind his eyes. "No, I am not a, ah, cop. But we'll talk later. You've lost a considerable amount of blood, but I think you can manage the walk. It's just to the edge of the park." His voice was coming through with a lot of static, like a transatlantic broadcast.

"I was just passing through on my way to the Greyhound station," I got the words out past a tongue like a sock full of sand. "Just point me that way and I'll drift out of your life."

He shook his head. "That's hardly safe, while the native wildlife is abroad. Just . . . along . . . my place . . . car . . ."
He was tuning in and out now; the static was getting worse on the short-wave band. I thought about lying down, but then my feet were working. He was towing me along and I gave up and followed, trying not to bump my head on my knees. I remember going under dark shrubbery, pushing through a hedge like a barbed-wire entanglement over what felt like dead men's bones but were probably just tree roots. Then I was getting helped into the seat of a small shiny car that looked like something hand-tooled for the King of Siam. It did a U-turn on a Kennedy dime and took off straight up. I knew then I was dreaming, so I leaned back into a seat upholstered with clouds and let it all slide.

CHAPTER TWO

Voices woke me. For a while I tried to ignore them, but something in the tone of the conversation made me prick up my ears.

One of the voices belonged to the little man from the park,

a couple of lifetimes ago. He sounded as though he had a nice glow working; or maybe he was just excited. The female voice was husky and low—lower than his—with an edge to it like a sawed board. It was saying:

". . . you're a fool to take a risk like this, Jess!"

"Minka, my dear, they have no way of knowing—"

"How do you know what they have? This is Death Control you're playing with now, not some two-cee meatlegger!"

I felt as dopey as a shanghaied deckhand, but I got an eyelid up, was looking at a high ceiling with ornate fretwork in gold and white. The walls under it were white, with little dabs of bright-colored tile here and there. There were a couple of chairs like pastel-toned eggshells perched on slim shiny rods, and a low table with a silver bowl half the size of a washtub, full of oversized bananas and pears, and grapes as big as golf balls. The floor was white, and there were silky-looking rugs spread on it.

I was lying on a neat little white bunk like a night nurse's cot, set up in a corner. My shirt was gone, and there was a layer of rubbery clear plastic over the six-inch slash in my side. I turned my head, not without a certain effort, and was looking past a row of columns along the far side of the room at blue sky that showed between them. Beyond the columns a terrace spread out, catching yellow sunlight. The little man was there, dressed in a pale pink suit with lace at the wrists. He was sitting in a violet chair worrying a fingernail.

The woman sitting with him was like something painted up to stand in front of a cigar store. Her hair was a varnished swirl of indigo, like a breaking wave, and there were faint orange spirals drawn on her cheeks, with the ends trailing down under her chin. Her outfit seemed to consist of a lot of colored ribbons, carelessly draped. All of this didn't disguise the fact that the bone structure was good enough to send a fashion photographer grabbing for his baby spots.

"You don't know who—or what—he might be," she was saying. "I thought your Secret Society had rules about picking up strangers."

"This is different! They were tracking him! They wanted him alive! Don't you see it?" The small man was waving both arms now. "If they *want* him—*I* want him!"

"Why do they want him?" she came back fast.

"I've admitted I don't know—yet. But you may be sure I'll find out. And then . . ."

"Then it's going to fall in on you, Jess! They don't bother with the rats in the dump—until one of them comes out and tries to steal the food off their plates."

Jess brought his hands up and made a clawing motion, as if he were shredding a curtain.

"Don't be a blind grub of a stupid Preke! After all these years, this is an opportunity—the first in my time—"

"I *am* a Preke." The woman's face was stiff as a plaster cast, and under the lacquer job, about the same color. "That's all I ever was—ever will be. And you're—what you are. Face it, Jess, make the best—"

"Accept this? From them?" Jess jumped up and raked at his chest as if he were trying to tear off a sign somebody had hung on him. "I could hold the universe in my hands!" He showed her his cupped palms. "But they—these upstarts who aren't fit to carry out my grandfather's garbage—they say 'no!'"

"You're not your grandfather, Jess."

"You'd preach to me, you bedizened Preke trollop!" He leaned across toward the woman and shook the backs of his hands at her. She lifted a corner of her mouth at him.

"I've liked you for what you are, Jess; the other never meant anything to me."

"You're a lying, scheming Preke slut!" Jess was screeching like a dry bearing now. "After all I've done to raise you from your filthy dirtside beginnings, when I need your help—"

"Be quiet, Jess. You'll wake him."

"Bah! I've shot him full of enough lethenol to paralyze a

platoon of Blackies. . . ." But he got up. I closed my eyes, listened to them come in and cross the floor to me. Neither of them said anything for half a minute.

"Caw, he's big enough," the woman said.

Jess tittered. "I had to strap two lift units to him to get him here."

"Was he badly hurt?"

"Just a nasty cut. I've given him two liters of blood, full spec with nutes."

"Why would they want anyone—alive?"

"He must know something." Jess sounded awed. "Something important."

"What could he know, that ETORP needs?"

"That's what I have to discover."

"You're a fool, Jess."

"Will you help me—or do you really intend to desert me, now that I need you?" Jess hissed the last words like a stepped-on snake.

"If it's what you want—of course I'll do what I can," the girl's voice was dull.

"Good girl. I knew you would . . ." Their feet went away. Something clicked and the room became very still. I opened my eyes again. I was alone.

2

For a while I lay where I was and looked at the fancy ceiling and waited for the memories to come flooding back; but nothing happened. I was still just Steve Dravek, former tough guy, once reputed to be a pretty savvy character but now not even sure what day it was or what continent I was on. Jess had sounded American, and so did the girl, but that didn't prove anything. The park could have been anywhere, and the street. . . . Well, in retrospect the street was a lot like something out of a dream fraught with obscure psychological significance. I wouldn't count the street.

Okay, Dravek; so where does that leave us?

In unfamiliar surroundings, broke, and nursing a knife wound—not a totally unique situation. I've come to in some pretty strange places in my time: from flophouses and fifty-cent dormitories where you could hear the crickets running footraces in the woodwork, to hundred-dollar-a-night suites with mink bath mats, where little lost ladies tapped discreetly at unexpected hours, trailing ninety-dollar-a-dram smells. A few times, I've started a day in a vacant lot with my pockets inside out; and now and then I've even awakened in a chintzy little bedroom with lots of hard morning sun shining in on the installment-plan furniture, showing up cracks in the wallpaper and flaws in complexions; and once I woke up in the hold of a Panamanian-registry banana scow sailing out of Mobile under a former Nazi destroyer skipper. He lived on mush for six weeks after I kicked in the door to his cabin and laid the schnapps bottle he was breakfasting from alongside his jaw. I was only seventeen at the time, but already pretty husky.

Yeah, I knew what it was like to wake up a little confused, throbbing a little here and there, with a mouth like an abandoned mouse nest and nothing but a set of raw knuckles and a fresh tattoo to help me reconstruct preceding events. But this time I didn't remember the celebration, or the cause for the celebration. What I did remember was an office paneled in dark, waxy wood, and a mean-looking old geezer with crew-cut white hair, nodding and saying, "Sure, Steve, if that's the way you want it."

Frazier. The name came slowly, like something remembered from a long time ago.

But what the hell—Frazier was my drinking buddy, a lean, wiry kid with bushy black hair and enough reach to spot most light-heavies ten pounds and a horseshoe . . .

But he was the old man, too. . . . I shook my head to get rid of the double exposure, and did some deep breathing. *Try again, Dravek.*

This time I got a big room like a blimp hangar, full of pipes and noise and sharp, sour smells. Lots of smoke in the air—or mist—and more mist rising from tanks like oversized oxygen bottles.

No help there. Once more.

This time I got a woman's face: high cheekbones, big dark eyes, red-brown hair that came down to slim shoulders, the willowy figure of a thoroughbred . . . but no name; no identity.

Come on, Dravek! You can do better than that: Address, phone number, occupation, last seen on the night of . . .

Back to that. I turned my head and was looking across the room at a flat black case, lying on the table by the door. It looked like a case with something in it.

Sitting up was hard work, but no harder than carrying a safe up a fire escape. The side gave signals, and I felt a warm, wet-diaper feeling against my ribs that meant something had ripped a little, but I got my feet on the floor and pushed. Nothing happened except for a little sweat popping out where my hackles would have been if I'd had any hackles. The next try was better; I was as heavy as a lead-lined casket but I made it across to the table. Coach called another time out then while I sat on the floor and pushed back a low fog that wanted to roll in over the scene. When my head cleared I went to work on the case.

It was rectangular, about two inches thick, six inches by eight, made of a soft, leathery material. My finger touched something and the top snicked back. I poked around in the kind of junk women have carted in handbags since Nefertiti's day. There was a long, curved comb, metal tubes of paint, a little box that rattled, some plastic shapes like charms for a charm bracelet, a folded paper that looked like a photostat of a magazine article. I opened it; except for the shorthand spelling, it read like a news item, written in the gushy tones of a fashion hack, all about the new Raped Look and the exciting corpse-colors that were taking the Crust by storm. There was nothing in that for me.

I started to toss it back and the line of print at the top caught my eye. It wasn't much, just a date: Sarday, Ma 33, 2103.

For a minute, the floor under my feet, the whole room, the city around me, seemed to turn to a thin gas, something my suppressed id had thought up during one of those long, hard nights just before the fever breaks.

"Twenty-one-oh-three," I said. "Ha—that's a good one." I dropped the paper on the floor and looked around at the room. It looked solid enough. There was a cool breeze moving in off the terrace now, and out beyond the columns I could see a couple of friendly-looking clouds. They had a nice familiar look that helped a lot just then.

"That makes next week my birthday," I said, but it didn't come out sounding cute. "My hundred and sixty-second . . ."

There wasn't much more I could do with that. I put the stuff back in the handbag and ate a couple of grapes to restore my strength and started checking the room.

There were three sealed openings in the wall that were probably doors, but poking and prodding didn't open them. I went out on the terrace and looked out across empty space at a couple of fanciful-looking towers poking up through a cloud layer maybe five hundred feet below. The drop from the balustrade was vertical. That didn't tell me much about where I was, except that it was a place I'd never heard of. I went back inside, prowled the wall near the bed where the tile patterns looked a little different, found a hairline crack, and leaned on it. Something clicked and a closet door popped open. I found a plain dark pullover to replace the shirt I'd been wearing. A drawer under the closet contained a supply of the kind of frilly items the little man called Jess would want next to his skin. I poked around under them, touched something cool and smooth. It looked like the offspring of an automatic and a mixmaster. I thought about taking it, but I wasn't sure which end the medicine came out of.

Another few minutes of scratching at the wall used up the rest of my energy, but netted me no more trophies. I ate one of the bananas and stretched out on the bed to wait. I listened to the wind flirting around the columns and tried to stay awake; but after a while I dropped off into a restless dream about a big room full of noise and excited faces, and a smaller room with smoke curling out past an open door, and a big tank, painted green. There was a man in a white uniform with blood on his face, and a woman, crying, and I was saying, "That's an order, damn your guts!" And then they were all backing away and I picked up the bundle in my arms and went in through the smoky door and heard behind me the sound of the woman, crying . . .

3

The sunny blue sky had turned to scarlet and purple before my host came back, humming a little tune between his teeth. The woman was with him. She left after a minute, and I played possum while he thumbed back my eyelid; then he went across to the wall and got busy poking buttons on a console that swung out on command. He took something out of a slot, held it up to the light and frowned at it, came back over to me and took hold of my arm. That was my signal to take hold of his neck. He squawked and flapped his arms and the thing in his hand hit the floor. I got my feet under me and stood up; he went for a pocket with one hand and I shifted grips and took him up against the wall. His eyes goggled at me.

"What have you got that's good for a lethenol hangover, Jess?" I leaned on him and let him get a swallow of air in past my thumb.

"Let me go . . ." It was thin squeak like a rubber rat.

"How long have I been here?"

"Thirty hours—but—"

"Who are you, Jess? What's your racket?"

"Are you . . . out of your mind? I saw you were in difficulty—"

"Why'd you butt in? It strikes me that park's rough territory for a little fellow like you."

He kicked and made choking sounds and I slacked off a little to let some of the purple drain out of his face.

He twisted his mouth into a grin like a wounded fox. "One has one's little hobbies," he got out, and tried to bite me. I pounded his head on the wall a few times. They both sounded solid. All this effort started my head humming again. "You're tough, Jess," I told him. "I'm tougher."

He tried with a finger for the eye, and I knocked him down and held him on the floor with a knee in his back and slapped his pockets. I found a couple of scented tissues and some plastic tokens. He said a few things, none of them helpful.

"You're making me curious, Jess," I tried to talk without panting. "It must be important dope you're hanging on to."

"If you'll take your thumb out of my throat so that we can talk together like civilized men, I'll tell you what I can. Otherwise, you may kill me and be damned to you!" He said it in a new voice, nothing like the whine he'd been using.

I let him sit up. "Let's start with who *they* are," I said. "The ones that wanted me alive."

"Blackies. Commission men." He spat the words.

"Make it plainer."

"Death Control, damn you! How plain does it have to be?"

"How do you know it's me they want?"

"I heard them talking. In the park."

"So you snatched me out from under their noses. What made me worth taking the chance?"

He tried out a couple of expressions, settled on a sad smile like a mortician suggesting a more appropriate tribute to a departed loved one.

"Really, you have a suspicious nature. I overheard nothing further than that they had seen you enter the park." He gave me a quick look. "By the way, how did *you* happen to be there?"

"I wandered in off the street. Maybe I was a little drunk."

He gave me a catty smile. He was getting his wind back fast. "I saw your work. Very clever—except for the carelessness just at the last."

"Yeah. Red fooled me."

"You would have bled to death."

I nodded. "Thanks for sticking me back together. That's one I owe you."

"How are you feeling now?" He cocked his head as if the answer was worth a lot of money and he didn't want to miss any overtones.

"Like it happened to two other guys. By the way, you wouldn't have a drink around the place?"

He looked at my hand holding his ruffled shirt. "May I?"

I stepped back and he got up and went past me to the alcove with the buttons, and punched a couple. He said "ah" and came back with a right-looking glass.

"Better get two."

He followed instructions. I traded glasses, watched him drink half of his, then tried mine. It tasted like perfumed apple juice, but I drank it anyway. Maybe it helped. My head seemed to clear a little. Jess dabbed the blood off his chin with a tissue. He got out a flat case and extracted a little cigaret no thicker than a matchstick, fitted it into a pair of little silver tongs, took a sip from it like a hummingbird sampling the first nectar of spring. He was looking relaxed now, as if we were old school chums having a cosy chat.

"You're a stranger here in the city," he said, making it casual. "Where do you come from?"

"Well, Jess, I have a little problem there. I don't exactly remember how I got to your town. I was hoping you might tell me."

He looked solemn and alert, like a sympathetic judge just before he hits you with the book. "I?"

"Our gentlemanly arrangement isn't going to work out unless you play, too, Jess."

"Really, you're asking the impossible," he said. "What would I know of you—a perfect stranger?"

I banged my glass on the table and leaned over and put my face an inch from his. "Try a guess," I said.

He looked me in the eye. "Very well," he said. "My guess is that you're an ice case, illegally out of low-O."

"What's that mean?"

"If I'm right," he said, "for the past hundred years or more, your body has been in an ETORP cryothesis vault—frozen solid at absolute zero."

CHAPTER THREE

Half an hour later, with a couple more innocent-tasting drinks under my belt, I was still asking questions and getting answers that made me ask more questions.

". . . most of the low-O's were placed in cold stasis by relatives: persons who were ill, with a then-incurable ailment—or injured in an accident. Their hope was that in time a cure would be found, and they'd be awakened. Of course, they never were. The dead stay dead. ETORP owns them now."

"I was never sick a day in my life. Outside of that, it sounds like a good story."

Jess shook his head. "The difficulty is that there hasn't been an authorized thaw for over fifty years, to my knowledge. And if you'd been revived under official sanction, you'd have awakened in an ETORP 'doc ward, with a cephalotaper clamped to your skull, pumping you full of a canned ETORP briefing, not wandering the streets in an amnesiac condition."

"Maybe a relative did the job."

"Relatives—of a corpse who's been on ice for a century? Not even your own great-great grandchildren would know anything of you—and if they did—would they give up their own visas for you?" Jess wagged his head. "And in any event, laws have been passed. We can't have the dead waking up, they tell us; there's no room for them, with a world population of twenty billion. And they cite the legal complications, hold up the specter of old diseases released. They make a good case, but the real reason is . . ." he looked at me, watching for my reaction. "Spare parts," he said crisply.

"Go on."

"Consider it!" He leaned toward me, slitted his eyes. "Perfectly good arms and legs and kidneys, going to waste—and outside—people needing them, dying for want of them! They're ready to pay ETORP's price, perform any service in return for life and health!"

"What's this ETORP?"

"Eternity, Incorporated."

"Sounds like a cemetery."

"A . . . ?"

"Where you bury the dead ones."

"The Blackies would gather you in for a trick like that." He sounded a little indignant. "The minerals are valuable, even if the hulk is useless."

"You were telling me about ETORP."

"ETORP controls the most precious commodity of all: life. It issues birth permits and life visas, performs transplants and cosmetic surgery, supplies rejuve and longevity treatments and drugs. Technically, it's a private corporation, operating under the Public Constitution. In fact, it rules our society with an iron hand."

"What about the government?"

"Pah! a withered organ, dangling anachronistically from the body politic. What power is there that compares with life? Money? Military force? What are they to a dying man?"

"Nice business. How did ETORP get the monopoly?"

"The company began simply enough, with patented drugs and techniques, invented in their own laboratories and closely controlled. Then they developed the frozen organ banks; then whole-body cryothesia. After the development of the cancer cures and the perfection of *ex utero* cultures, there was a last-ditch legal fight with a group calling themselves the Free Life party. They charged the company with murder and abortion, sacrilege, desecration of the dead, all manner of crimes. They lost, of course. The bait ETORP had to dangle over judges' heads was irresistible. After that, ETORP's power burgeoned at geometric rates. It bought and sold legislators like poker chips. It became a tyrant that ruled with a whip in one hand and a sweet in the other! And all the while, its vaults were filling with freeze cases, waiting for a resurrection that would never come."

"So old Uncle Elmer never woke up after all . . ."

"So sad," Jess said. "All those trusting souls, saying goodbye, kissing their children and wives and going off to the hospital, leaving pitiful little notes to be opened on anniversaries, going under the anesthetic babbling of the parties they'd stage when they came back . . . and now—a century later—sawed apart to be sold from open stock to the lucky ones with negotiable skills, or handed out as door prizes to faithful company hacks. And bodies! Whole bodies, an almost unlimited supply, something that had never been plentiful. That was where the power was, Steve—that was what made ETORP! What was a billion dollars to a ninety-year-old mummy in a wheelchair? He'd pay it all for a twenty-year-old body—possibly keeping a million or two in reserve for a new stake."

"Maybe I'm slow. What good would a dead body do him?"

"Dead?" Jess's eyebrows went up. "It's the *living* body that's valuable, Steve. A young hulk, cured of its once-fatal ailments, will fetch its weight in graymarket chits." I was still frowning at him, and he added, "For brain transfer, you understand."

"Do I?"

He looked surprised. "There are always wealthy Crusters and Dooses with lapsed visas. For a price, it's easy enough to arrange new papers—but those are worthless to a man with a dying body. And prime hulks are in short supply. Dirties won't do, of course; riddled with defects."

"You're talking about scooping out a man's brains and putting somebody else's in?"

"Even in your day the surgical transplant of limbs and organs was practiced. The brain is simply another organ."

"OK; so I'm wanted by the law for illegally rising from the dead. Where does that leave us? Who thawed me? And why?"

Jess thought about it for three puffs of his dope stick. "Steve —how old were you—*are* you?"

I felt the question over in my mind. I had the feeling the answer was on the tip of my tongue, but I couldn't quite pin it down. "About fifty," I said. "Middle-aged."

Jess got up and went across to a table, came back with a hand mirror with an ivory handle.

"Look at yourself."

I took the mirror. It was a good glass, nine inches square. It showed me a face that was mine, all right; but the hairline was an inch lower on the forehead than it should have been, and the lines I'd collected in a lot of years of trying to pound the world into submission with my head were gone like the shine on five-dollar shoes. I looked like a new recruit for the freshman grid squad, turned down for underage.

2

"Tell me about yourself, Steve," Jess said. "Anything at all. Start at the beginning—your earliest memories."

"I remember the early days all right. My childhood, if you can call it that." I rubbed the side of my face and tried to think about it, but the ideas that should have been ready to jump into my mind felt rusty and old, as if I hadn't thought about them, hadn't used the words, for a long, long time.

"I was kicked up in a tough part of Philly, went to sea, joined the Army when the Chicoms busted loose in Burma. After the war I went to school, got enough education to start in as a white-collar man with a grocery chain. Five years later, I owned the company . . ." I listened to myself talking, remem-

bering it all in a vague, academic sort of way, as if it was something I saw in the movies.

"Go on."

"The office; the plant. A big car with two telephones . . ."
Shadowy memories were taking shape; but there was something dark there I didn't like.

"What else?" Jess whispered.

"I remember my days at sea better." This was a safer subject;
I was talking to myself now, looking into the past. "That was
real: The stinks and the rust on the deck and the mold growing
on my shore shoes, and coastlines in the morning like white
reefs coming out of the mist, and the noise and the lights in
port at night, and the waterfront joints and the lousy booze and
the guy that used to play sad tunes on the fantail after the
hatches were down."

"It sounds quite romantic."

"Like a case of the yaws. But it had a certain something;
something to do with being young and tough, sleep anywhere,
eat anything, fight anybody . . ."

"Tell me about your business associates. Perhaps one of
them . . ." he let it trail off. I thought about it, tried to sort out
the conflicting impressions. A young fellow with black hair; an
old bird with a neck like a turkey . . .

"My best pal was a fellow I served with in China and Nepal.
He saved my life once; plugged the hole in my wrist where a
Chink .25 mm went through." I remembered it all: The two-
mile walk back to the forward aid station, handling the BAR
left-handed while the woods buzzed with scatter-shell fragments; the surgeons clucking like hens and then settling down
to three hours of needlework that would have won prizes at
the county fair, while Frazier poured slugs for both of us and
kept my cigar lit. They'd done a nice job of putting nerves and
blood vessels back together, but the carpal joint was never the
same, and there was an inch-wide scar that was the reason I'd
taken to wearing my Rolex Oyster on my left wrist. . . . I had
a sudden idea, one that had been ducking around the edge of

my consciousness, flapping its arms for attention ever since I
woke up in the rain.

I flipped my cuff back and looked at the wrist. The skin was
unflawed. The scar was gone.

"What is it?" Jess was watching my face. I turned the cuff
back down.

"Nothing. Just another little slip in my grip on reality. What
would you say to another shot of what we just had?"

He watched me while I poured out a nice jolt. I took it
back without bothering to roll it on my tongue.

"This freezing process," I said. "Does it remove scars?"

"Why, no—"

"Does it make you look younger?"

"Nothing of that sort, Steve—"

"Then scratch your theory."

"What do you mean?"

"If I was one of your freeze cases, I'd remember a brick wall
running at me, or a sickbed and a flock of medicine bottles
and some old goat shaking his whiskers and saying, 'Ice this
boy until I figure out what to do next.'"

Jess pushed his lips in and out. "It's quite possible that the
trauma associated with the shock—"

"It wasn't an accident; no scars, remember? And if I had a
fatal ailment—who cured it?"

He looked a little nervous. "Perhaps you weren't cured."

"Relax, cancer's not catching."

"Steve—this is no joking matter! We have to find out who you
are, what you know that makes you a threat to ETORP!"

"I'm no threat. I'm just a mixed-up guy who wants to get
unmixed and back to minding my own business."

"They're afraid of you! Nothing else could explain a class Y
search for you—and therein lies a weapon to be used against
them!"

"If you're talking revolution, count me out."

"Count you out—on the quest for the greatest prize the
world has ever known?"

"What are you dancing around the edge of, Jess?"

His eyes went to slits with a glint back of them like Midas thinking about Fort Knox.

"Immortality."

"Sure. Throw in flying carpets while you're at it."

"It's no myth, Steve! They have it! It's there, don't you understand? We don't have to die! We could live forever! But will they share it with us? No, they let us toil and die like grubs in an ant heap!"

"You toil, Jess? Don't tickle me; my side still hurts."

"Longevity treatments, rejuve!" Jess spat out the words like a dirty taste. "A sop for the tech class they need to keep their corrupt machine functioning! Limb and organ graft and regeneration—and the ultimate iniquity, brain transfer, and the attendant black market in bodies that makes it unsafe for an unarmed man to walk abroad at night. And all in order to keep up the value of their stock-in-trade!"

"Times haven't changed much," I said. "In my day it was Zionist plots and pills you could drop in the gas tank to convert water to gasoline."

"You think I'm raving? Consider it, Steve! Medical research long ago synthesized protoplasm, created life in the laboratory, cured cancer—and in the process, inevitably discovered the secret of the aging process! It's a disease, like any other—and they've cured it! Nature doesn't care, you see; her intent was only to preserve the individual past the breeding age. Fifteen years to sexual maturity, another fifteen years of vigorous life to see the next generation on the way—then—decay! Just as we've begun to learn to live, we begin to die! No wonder the race lives in anarchy and turmoil, each generation repeating the mistakes of the one before! The world is run by children, while our mature minds, seasoned by life, go down to death. And they could stop it!"

"How could they keep a thing like that a secret—if they had it?"

"By limiting its use to a favored few—in whose interest it would be, of course, to preserve the deception."

"Uh-huh—but somebody would notice after a while if old Mr. Gotrocks never showed up in the obit column."

"Who? Who keeps records of such things? It's not as it was in your day, Steve; we have no public figures as you knew them; we live in a rigidly stratified society; Dooses know little of the activities of Crusters; Threevees never venture down to Forkwaters; and no graded citizen ever sets foot dirtside, among the visaless Preke rabble."

"That's all guesswork, Jess. Why get excited about it—"

"There are those of us who feel that man wasn't meant to die in his prime, Steve! It's not his destiny! Life eternal is almost in our grasp—life in which to see the stars and the planets and the riches thereof—"

"Seventy years are long enough. I won't waste 'em chasing a pot of gold at the end of a cardboard rainbow."

"Seventy years?" Jess popped his eyes at me. "I'm seventy-nine now!" His voice broke. "I expect to live to a hundred and fifteen, even without the blessing of ETORP! But there's more, Steve—so much more—and that's where you can help!"

"Sorry—I've got other plans."

"Plans? You, a nobody without even an identity?"

Just then, as if it had been waiting for the signal, a cool chime cut through the still of the evening.

3

Jess came out of his chair like a cocky featherweight answering the bell for Round 2. All his teeth were showing in a grin that had no humor in it. The tone sounded again, twice, three times.

"Minka?" Jess asked the air.

The chime stopped and somebody pounded on the door.

"Just like old times," I said. "That sounds like copper to me, Jess."

"How could they . . . ?" he started and then closed his mouth. He gave me a narrow-eyed look.

"You can trust me now," he said, "or not, just as you please. Neither of us wants you found here. There's one way out for us."

"What have you got in mind?"

"Out there." He pointed to the terrace. "I'll give them something to think about. What you do is up to you." He didn't wait to catch my reaction, just started across toward the door. That left me a couple of seconds to think it over. I looked around, saw three blank walls and the columns leading to the terrace. I went out, stood in the shadows.

Jess opened the door—and was backing into the room, holding his hands out from his sides. A man was pushing him, and another was behind, looking as happy as his kind of face could. They were lean, slim-hipped lads, buckled into black uniforms with silver cord down the pants seams and more silver worked into their stiff stand-up collars. They wore holsters strapped down low, in working position, and their eyes had that screw-you-Jack look that spelled cop or professional soldier as far as you could hear a pair of heels click.

"Say all the right things," one of them said in a filed-steel voice, "and you could live to cash in your chits."

"What's all this?" Jess sounded a little breathless. "My visa is in order—"

The cop backhanded him down onto the floor.

"Topside wants you bad," the cop nodded. "I guess this is the first clean spring from the Palace in sixty years. Now, let's have it all: How you handled the outer ring, how you took the main vault, who did the thaw job—the works."

Jess was sitting up, looking tearful. "You're making a mistake—"

The Blackie hit him. Jess curled up on the rug and made noises like a lonely pup.

"Start now and save muscle all around," the Blackie said. "Who was your first contact?"

Jess looked up at him. "He was a big fellow, about seven-three, with chin whiskers and a glass eye," he said in a nasty tone. "I didn't get the name."

"Funny man." The Blackie swung his foot and caught Jess in the shoulder as he rolled away. The other cop kicked him back.

"Where's the other one at?"

They fanned out and looked at the bare walls. One of them blew air out over his lower lip and looked at his partner.

"I thought you had this pile staked off."

"Maybe the mothering crot's got an outlaw shaft."

"He couldn't have used it. Power block, remember?"

"We should have called this in, Supe."

I backed a quiet step; a light breeze moved palm fans in a pot beside me. They weren't big enough to help much. The boys inside didn't look any smarter than their kind usually do, but after a while it was going to occur to them to take a peek out on the back porch.

"Then he couldn't have got out—" one of the cops said, and stopped. I could almost hear his brains working: If there were two guys in a locked room and only one in sight, how many are still hiding under the rug?

I thought about stepping out and trying the honest citizen routine, but those guns the boys packed looked big and impatient. And even if I didn't buy Jess's program a hundred percent, there were a couple of things about this pair that put me on the other side.

"I don't like it, Supe," the number two cop was saying. "We shouldn't of played wise with a Y priority."

"There's twenty-year chits in it for the ones that take him solo . . ." The voices were keeping up the patter, coming my way. I blinked sweat out of my eyes and waited. What I needed was a break, one lousy little break. It was too much to ask for, too much to expect from a frail-looking little fellow who had already absorbed more punches than a Golden Gloves runner-up losing the big one. But something about the little I'd seen of Jess made me set myself and get ready . . .

When it came, it was a bleat like a docked sheep. "I'll tell you! Why should I lose my visa for that mothering weed?"

The feet held up and then went back and I eased over to the right and faded an eye past the edge of the open door. Jess was on his feet. What was holding him there was the boss Blackie. He was standing with his back to me. He had his legs planted well apart and was holding a handful of Jess's pretty green shirt in his left fist and bending him backward over the table. There was a lot of blood on the little man's face, and one eye was swollen almost shut. The other cop was leaning against the wall to the right. If he had moved his eyes an eighth of an inch he'd have been looking straight at me. I stayed where I was and waited.

"We got all night," the cop said. "Tell it now or tell it in an hour, we don't care. We like our work."

Jess mumbled something, but I wasn't paying much attention to the conversation. What I was watching was Jess's right hand. It was feeling over the table, out of sight of the other cop. The fingers worked carefully, deliberately, as though they had all the time in the world. They teased the drawer open, came out with the tip of a thin blade between them. The fingers worked the knife around until they could touch the narrow black-taped grip, closed over it. Jess's arm came up slowly, carefully, poised for a moment with the needletip just touching the black cloth stretched over the ribs of the man bending over him. Then with a smooth thrust, he put it in.

The Blackie jerked once, as if he had touched something hot. He pivoted slowly, still holding Jess.

"What are you doing?" his partner took a step toward him. The cop's hand went to his side, caressed the knife hilt that was tight against the black cloth. Then his knees went, and he hit the floor hard. The other Blackie came forward a step, raked at the gun at his hip, and I was into the room and behind him. He was slow turning and I hit him in the neck, twice, and he dropped the gun and jackknifed to the floor and lay twisted, the way they do when the spine is shattered.

I kicked the gun across the room and Jess staggered away from the table, breathing with a lot of noise. I looked at the door.

"They came alone," Jess gasped it out. He wiped blood off his mouth. "They were keeping this play to themselves. Nice for us, Steve. No one knows where they were." He made a face and I saw he was grinning.

"You're a great actor," I said. "What do you do for an encore?"

"We make a good team," he said. "A pity to break it up."

I went over to the bar and poured myself a stiff one and swallowed it.

"Let's put this pair in the back closet," I said. "Then get a map of New York City, circa 1970. I think I may have an idea."

CHAPTER FOUR

The map on the tabletop screen showed the eastern half of the state plus a chunk of Pennsylvania and Jersey. The highway grid looked a lot denser than it should have, but otherwise it was pretty normal. The date in the corner was 1992.

"Higher mag," I said, and he focused down until the city filled the screen. I asked him to center it on Long Island, the Jamaica section, and he worked the knobs and got a blowup that showed every street and major building. I pointed to a spot. "That's it: my old plant."

"And you imagine that would be intact today? The building probably doesn't exist—"

"The spot I'm looking for wasn't exactly in a building, Jess. It was under one—a place that was built to last. I made some arrangements for that."

"You think you might have left some clue there?"

"It's a place to look."

He poked a lever. A red dot popped up at the top of the

screen, and he used two knobs to guide it down to mark the plant. Then he blanked the screen and a new map came onto it. It looked like one of those webs built by a drunk spider. There were cryptic symbols all over it like Chinese alphabet soup. Jess looked up at me. There was a strange look in his eye.

"Interesting spot you've picked," he said. "This is a cartogram of modern Granyauck, overlying the site of the town you used to know. As you'll notice, the former islands have been joined to the mainland by various hydraulic works. The section you call Long Island, here . . ." he pointed to a green blob that covered a piece of the screen— "is an ETORP reserve. The specific point in which you expressed an interest happens to coincide almost precisely with the most closely guarded premises in the North American Sector."

"What is it?"

"The Cryothesis Center," he said. "Vulgarly known as the Ice Palace." He smiled. "I think we've made a connection, Steve."

2

Jess was pacing the floor. "It poses an interesting problem, Steve. I won't say it can't be done—I pride myself on my ability to enter presumably closed precincts—but the question remains —is it worth the risk involved?"

"If you want to back out, I'll go in alone."

"I'd like nothing better than to back out." He looked at me and I thought he looked a little pale around the jaw. "But as you said, it's our only lead. Therefore, the question is: How best to beard ETORP in his stronghold?"

He went back to his fancy desk and punched more keys, spent the next hour muttering at technical diagrams that were over my head like the Goodyear blimp.

"The Hudson outfall appears the likeliest spot," he said. "That means going dirtside, but it can't be helped."

"When do we start?"

"As soon as your wound has knit. And it will be as well for you to stay out of sight for a few days. After a century, that shouldn't matter much."

I conceded the point.

We ate then, and afterward sat out on the terrace and listened to music, some of it old enough to sound familiar. Then he showed me to a room papered with black roses and I stretched out in a shaft of moonlight and after a while slid down into a dream about a small pale face behind a pane of frosted glass and the vague shadows of forgotten sorrows as remote as a pharaoh's last wish.

3

We waited three days to make our move; my side was still tender, but Jess's medicine had healed it to a thin scar.

He fitted me out with a set of shiny black long johns that turned out to be lightweight scuba gear and led the way by back routes down into the depths of the city to a high blank wall with lights far up on it and that grim look that prisons and military installations have.

"This is the outer perimeter wall of the reserve," Jess said. I looked up at the top, fifty feet up in deep shadow.

"How do we get over it?"

"We don't, of course. We circumvent it. Come along."

I trailed him to the end of the alley, and we were facing a chest-high wall with lots of dark, cold air beyond it. I looked over it, saw black water swirling twenty feet below.

"A pleasant evening for a swim," Jess said. He pulled off his jacket and produced a slim-barreled gun from somewhere and made clicking sounds with it, checking the action. I stripped down to my frogman suit and turned up the heat control a notch higher. Jess looked me over to be sure I hadn't left my seat flap hanging down, and vaulted up on the coping of the wall, agile as a squirrel.

"Stay clear of the rungs when you dive," he said. "And be

sure to keep your comset open. Its range is only about a hundred feet, under water." He gave me a casual wave, like a movie star dismissing a fan, and tilted over the edge. I hopped up on the wall, swung both legs over, and kicked off without looking, feet-first.

4

It seemed like a long fall before I hit water as hard as a sidewalk and felt myself tumbling in a strong current that sucked the heat out of me like a blotter. I straightened myself out facing upstream and looked for Jess. It was like swimming in an inkwell. I found my heat control and thumbed it up, then tried my water jets.

"Use more power," Jess's voice tinned very faintly in my left ear. "You're drifting off."

I found the controls and used them and Jess guided me his way. When I was three feet from him, I saw the faint phosphorescent outline of his suit. He was hanging onto a mossy pipe projecting from the retaining wall.

"We have a brisk little swim ahead of us," he told me. "The duct I was hoping to use is blocked, but there should be another, a hundred and forty meters upstream."

It was a half-hour battle. Once I angled out a little too far and the tide took me and rolled me half a dozen times before I got my keel under me again. After a while the wall beside me changed from mossy concrete to rusted metal.

"Steer for the lights," Jess transmitted. A minute or two later, I saw a greenish arc glowing off to my right that turned out to be the open mouth of a six-foot conduit. There were some symbols painted on it in luminous pink and a mechanism bolted to the side. Jess was perched on the housing, tinkering. I heard him say "ah" and the louvers that blocked the mouth pivoted and I could see light coming from inside the duct. Water was boiling out of it like a millrace. He headed in, using the hand rungs, and I followed. The miniature pump strapped to my back hummed and the straps sawed under my arms. We passed up a pair of side branches and the duct narrowed. There was a glow-strip along the side here, with more symbols. Jess checked each one we came to, after a while held up and said, "There should be a hatch here."

I flattened myself against the curved wall and held on and watched while he checked over the section ahead. Then his head and shoulders disappeared. I came up beside him and his legs went up inside a vertical shaft a yard in diameter. There were rungs there. I hauled myself up after him and after ten feet, the shaft angled and we were coming out of water into open air.

5

"I suppose this is a maintenance lock," Jess said. It was a square room, twenty feet on a side, with motor-operated valves all over one wall and color-coded piping on the other ones. I could hear pumps throbbing somewhere. The ceiling shed a glow like phosphorescent mold on Jess's face. In the tight black suit, he looked like a detail from Hieronymus Bosch.

I was looking at a panel set between banked valves.

"Try this," I said.

Jess looked at me, said nothing. He unclipped a tool kit from his belt and went to work. Five minutes later he grinned at me and turned something slowly and the look of strain tightened. Beyond the wall, something made a solid snick.

"That's it," he said.

I went past him and pushed on the panel and a section of wall slid back and I was looking into a silent corridor with a row of green ceiling lights that stretched away into distance.

"So much for the impregnability of ETORP," Jess said. "We're inside the Ice Palace. There are a thousand Blackies patrolling a few feet overhead, but we seem to have this level to ourselves. Now what?"

I didn't answer him right away. I was looking at the corridor, and feeling little icy fingers running up my backbone.

"Did you ever walk into a strange place and have the feeling you'd been there before?" I spoke carefully, so as not to shatter a fragile thought.

"It's called the *déjà vu*," Jess said, watching me.

"There's something down there," I said. "Something I won't like."

"What is it, Steve?" Jess's voice was like a freezing man breathing on the dying spark of his last match.

"I don't know," I said. I looked along the hall, but it was just a hall now. I pointed toward the far end.

"Come on, Jess," I said. "I don't know whether it's a hunch or a nightmare, but I think what we want's that way."

6

"There's dust here," Jess said. "This section's not in use, hasn't been for a long time."

The corridor ran for a couple of hundred feet and ended in a right-angle turn with a cubbyhole full of shelves. There was nothing on them but dust. Under the shelves there was a row of hooks designed for coats, but no coats were hanging on them. Jess stamped on the floor, looked at the ceiling.

"There must be a route leading from here," he said. "This appears to be a dressing room, where special protective clothing was donned."

I was looking at the hooks. Something about them bothered me. I counted them. Twelve. I got a grip on the third from the right and pulled down. It felt pretty solid. I pushed up hard, and it clicked and folded back. Jess was watching me with his mouth open. I fingered the next one, then took hold of the fifth in line, flipped it up. I could feel a little sweat on my forehead under the mask. I reached for the hanger between the other two and lifted it and something made a crunching sound and the wall on the right jumped open half an inch.

"How did you know, Steve?"

"I don't know," I said, and pushed the door open and went through into a place I'd seen somewhere, a long time ago, in a dream of another life.

7

It was a wide room with walls that were cracked and water-stained, with green mold growing in little tufts along the cracks. There were cracks across the floor, too, and some curled chips of perished plastic were all that was left of the composition tiles. I saw this by the light of a small hand flash that Jess played over the floor and held on a door across the room.

I went across to it and turned the old-fashioned doorknob and went into a small office drifted half an inch deep in dust and scraps of paper as brown as autumn leaves. There was a collapsed jumble of leather scraps and rusted springs in one corner that had been a big chair. Across from it was a teakwood desk. There was a small bowl on the desk with a little dust at the bottom, and a shred of something that might have been a flower stem, once.

"Daisies," I said. "White daisies."

"Steve, do you know this place?" Jess whispered.

"It's my old plant," I said. "This was my office."

I went to the desk, opened the drawer, and took out a bottle. A scrap of label read EMY ARTIN.

"What else do you remember, Steve?"

I was looking at a picture frame hanging on the wall. The glass was dirty but intact, but there was nothing behind it but a little ash. I lifted it down and uncovered a steel plate with a round knob, set in the wall. It was a safe, and the door was ajar.

"Someone's been here before you," Jess's voice grated.

I reached far back in the safe and felt over the upper surface, found a pinhole. "I need a wire," I said. Jess checked a pouch at his belt and produced one. I poked it up in the hole and it snicked and the back of the safe tilted forward into my hand. There was a drawer behind it. I pulled it out. Except for a few flakes of dry black paint, it was empty.

8

"What did you expect to find here?" Jess asked me.

"I don't know." I blew into the empty steel box and the paint chips danced and whirled up into my face. I started to toss it aside and found myself looking at the bottom of the drawer. The paint there was dry, peeling.

"What is it?" Jess was watching my face.

"There was no paint on the inside," I said. "It's black carballoy . . ." I picked at the paint with a fingernail, and more of it flaked away and I was looking at words etched in the hard metal:

IN THE SEALED WING.

9

. . . *Frazier was looking at me with the kind of look you give a dog that's been run over. Gatley was standing behind him and Smith and Jacobs and a couple of men from the maintenance shop.*

"Follow your orders, damn you!" I was yelling, and the blood was thudding in my temples like nine-pound sledges. "I told you to wall it off, and by God I meant I wanted it walled off! I never want sunlight to shine in there again!"

"We all know how you feel, Steve," Frazier was saying. "But there's no use—"

Hobart pushed up beside him and his fat face came open and said, "Look here, Dravek, we have fifty thousand dollars invested in this project—"

I swung on him and somebody tried for my arms from behind and I broke his leg and then they were all backed against

*the wall in a bunch but Frazier, who was always the only one
with the guts to face me. There was blood on his mouth. A me-
chanic named Brownie was on the floor, groaning.*

*"He's gone crazy!" Hobart was yelling, and Frazier was look-
ing me in the eye and saying, "All right, Steve, if that's what
you want . . ."*

10

"Do you know what it means?" It seemed like a long time
had passed, but Jess was still standing beside me with the light
in his hand and I was holding the box. I tossed it on the floor
and the clatter was muffled in the dust.

"Yeah," I said. "I know." I went back out into the outer room.
The egg-crate ceiling was a dark tapestry of sooty spider webs
and the walls that had been a soft tan were blackish-green,
but I knew the way now. On the far side, a door was set in an
alcove beside a rusty pipe pushing up from the rotted casing of
a water cooler. It squeaked and opened and Jess's light showed
us another room, full of dust and age and piles of shapeless
debris where chairs and tables had been.

"Waiting room," I said. "Receptionist's desk over there." I
went past the jumble of rusted-out metal and along a hall
where dust came up in clouds, through a pair of doors that
fell off their hinges when I kicked them and down steps to a
pair of rusted steel doors that were standing open.

I looked at the doors, feeling the kind of feeling that Petrie
must have had when he read the inscription over King Tut's
tomb. My pulse was slamming, slow and heavy, a funeral
march. I didn't want to see what was on the other side. I took a
deep breath and Jess came down beside me and put the light
inside. It made long shadows in a wide, high room, with piping
and fallen scaffolding along one wall and a half-completed
framework of steel plating looming up in the background like a
wrecked tanker. There was lots of dust here, too, and a faint
rotten smell in the air.

Jess's light fingered the wall ahead, flicked up along the side of the big tank, showed up piping and condensers and power transformers rafter-mounted up under the black ceiling.

"What was it all for?" Jess asked. "What sort of work did you do here?"

"We were a food packaging and processing outfit. The big tank was part of a new process we developed."

"Why wasn't it completed?"

"I don't remember."

Jess played the light around some more, and held it on the floor. Footprints in the dust led toward the far wall. They skirted a coil of heavy cable with cracked insulation, went on into shadows. My face felt clammy and the palms of my hands were numb. There was something waiting for me up ahead and the fear of it was like cold lead in my stomach. I stepped off, following the trail, and Jess came behind, lighting the way.

11

On the other side of the big unfinished tank there was a deep bay with a railed gallery. I went up the companionway, along past open-sided cubicles with stainless steel tubs, still bright under the dust. The stink was stronger here. The footprints turned in at the last bay. I ducked under the low hood, and stopped that way, bent over, looking through a framed opening that had been made by tearing out a wall. The light made complicated shadows across a room full of machinery. Cables and tubes and pipes led from the apparatus to a ten-foot tank like an iron lung. A hatch at one end of the tank was standing open. I could see something inside; something that took hold of my guts like a giant bird's claw and squeezed. I reached and swung the door back and the thing inside glided out on a white porcelain slab and I was looking down at a man's face, dry and brown as carved wood, with shaggy, dry hair, sandy brown, and a glint of teeth showing at the edge of the withered lips.

CHAPTER FIVE

The body was nothing but purplish-brown leather stretched over bones. There were a couple of dozen tiny wounds visible on the skin.

"This is a life-support tank," Jess said. "It's been sabotaged. See the broken wires?"

"This is just a kid," I said. "Not more than sixteen years old. The hair's long, but there's no sign of a beard."

"He appears to have desiccated perfectly in the sterile atmosphere."

"The guy that sent us here didn't do it just to show us this," I said. "There's got to be more. Give me a hand."

I took hold of the right arm; it felt as hard and dry as last year's corn husks, and about as heavy. There was nothing under the cadaver except a blackish stain on the porcelain.

Jess played the light inside the tank, showed up a tangle of conduits and wires. The body was on its back, one leg drawn up a little, the arms at the sides, the fists closed. One fist looked a little different than the other. I bent over and looked.

"He's got something in his hand," I said. I broke off one of the fingers getting it out. It was a metal tube three inches long, half an inch in diameter. There was a screw cap at one end. I twisted it off and pulled out tightly rolled papers.

I unrolled them and a couple of faded newspaper clippings slid out into my hand. I smoothed the top one out and read it:

> Police today continued their investigation into the mystery surrounding the discovery of an unidentified body in a midtown hotel late yesterday. Although the apparent cause of death was suicide from a small-caliber gas gun, a small wound in the roof of the mouth indicated possible foul play. The victim, apparently in his late thirties, was

dressed in the uniform of a major in the UN Constabulary. UN Headquarters has so far declined to comment. (IP)

The next one was a bigger spread, two long columns in small, crabbed type that had a familiar look to it. The headline read: MAN GUNNED IN DAYLIGHT MURDER. The story under it told me that just before press time a gray Monojag had pulled up to the Waldorf and a man in the back seat had poked a 6mm Bren gun out the window and fired a full clip into a man in a brown overcoat coming out the revolving door. An employee of the hotel had been slightly injured in the knee by a ricochet. Examination of the body failed to produce any indication of the identity of the murdered man. The Monojag had driven off and made good its escape. Police were following up several clues and expected to make an arrest at any moment.

I handed the clip to Jess and another one dropped. I picked it up and was looking at a picture of myself.

It wasn't a bad likeness, except that it showed a little more hair than seemed just right, and there was a small scar high on the right cheekbone that didn't look familiar. And there was something wrong with the expression. But the part that hit my nervous system like a fire hose full of ice water was the caption:

BODY IGNORED BY PASSENGERS

The lines below read:

Civil Peace Under-Commissioner Arkwright announced today that record search has so far failed to identify the visaless body discovered late yesterday in Mid-city Tube Central.

The corpse, which had been ignored for several hours by Tube patrons who assumed the man was sleeping, is thought to be that of a criminal sought by Peace authorities for violation of the Life Act. See story page 115.

2

"What is it?" I said. "A gag, or a fake, or little slip in the editorial department?"

Jess was reading the clip. He didn't answer. I looked at the picture some more. It was me, all right; and something about it bothered me . . .

"This is no fake," I said. "The guy in the picture was dead when they took it, all right."

Jess glanced at the photo. "Why do you say that?"

"You prop the body up, get the eyelids open, and set the lights to give you a little reflection off the eyeball, tuck the tongue back inside and run a comb through the hair. It looks OK—unless you know what to look for. The Chicoms used to use the trick to keep the Red Cross happy about the prisoners."

"Horrible. Still, since he was dead when they found him, I suppose it's understandable."

"Maybe I'm a little slow. Back where I come from, a fellow doesn't often get a look at his own obituary."

Jess gave me his pained look. "You talk as if you imagined that was a picture of yourself."

"Imagine, hell! I know a picture of me when I see it."

"The coincidence in appearance *is* rather striking—"

"Ha!"

"The clips could refer to relatives of yours. Perhaps it's a vendetta—a rather fantastic vendetta, I confess—"

"It's a swell theory," I cut him off. "Except that I don't know anything about a feud, and I never had a twin."

"You had a grandfather."

"Make that a little plainer."

"Take another look at the date on the clip," he said. "It's over sixty years old."

3

My face felt like something chipped out of ice, but I pushed it into a grin.

"That clears that up. I'm not a fresh corpse on a slab down at the city morgue; I'm a nice settled cadaver who's been pushing up daisies the bigger half of a century."

Jess nodded as if that meant something. Maybe it did. I was still hanging in the air feeling for the floor with my toes. There was another paper back of the clips. Jess put the light on it while I unrolled it. It was covered with typing. I smoothed it out on the side of the tank and read it:

Number Three gave me most of it. The major almost had it, but he slipped somewhere and they took him. He had the best chance of any of us. Less time had gone by and the organization he was up against wasn't as solid yet, and his taping was better. He spent ten years getting ready, but they nailed him. Three had a tough time, but he picked up his cues and carried it a little farther, and from what he found out gave me the tip that brought me here. But none of it would have happened except for Frazier. He was the only man that could have handled the Plan. He knew what he was doing when he picked him for the job.

What I'm going to try may not work, and if it doesn't, I'll wind up like the major and this poor kid here who never even had a name. But it's what I have to do. Maybe I'm wasting my time writing long chatty letters to a guy that doesn't exist, never will exist. But I'm banking on it that I'm not the last. OK, you read the note Number Three left, and came here, just like I did. The box was empty when I found it, too, but his tip to try the sealed wing was there. The paint I put back over it won't last more than ten years, and that ought to be long enough—unless *he* finds you first. But that's where he outfoxed himself.

Maybe the old devil knew himself better than he thought he did. The story about making the setup torture proof was a little far-fetched. He couldn't afford to let himself know. Maybe he even saw this coming some day. But if he did, why—[word scratched out].

To hell with that. Let's keep this short. I've got plenty of time, my trail's covered and cold, maybe he thinks I'm dead. I tried hard enough to make him think so. Five years I've laid doggo now. But now it's time to move. Can't stall forever. Because I found it.

It's a place you know—but maybe you don't. The systems are getting old. There are gaps in my briefing. Number Three said there might be. He had it all, right up to the beginning of the Plan. I remember the trial, and the start of the project, but it all seems a little academic, like a story you've heard too many times. Or it did. Now that I've seen what I have, it eats at me. I haven't had eighty years to forget, like he has. But now I'm ready to make my try. Maybe he'll be ready for me, and I'll wash up on a beach a thousand miles from there. But I've got to try it now, before I get any rustier. Maybe I've already waited too long, but I had to wait, give myself every break there was—because if I fail, there may not be a Number Five.

Funny how I can't stick to the point. I guess I want to talk to somebody; but there's nobody a man can trust. ETORP's stranglehold is getting tighter every day. Now they have private cops with little black lapel badges crawling every street in the city, and there's a lot of talk about some kind of legalized euthanasia, with ETORP running it on a contract deal. Some organization. Maybe I ought to feel proud; maybe I do, in a way. But I'll break it, or get killed. I hope I make it. I've got to make it. It may be the last chance. Just on the off chance something goes wrong, I'm leaving this for you. If anybody else finds this it's got to be him, and what good is a code with him? You'll know what to do with it. And if you don't, you've forgotten too much—or never got it—

It's too complicated for me. Things moved fast after my

day. We would have called it magic, and maybe it is. Black
magic. Bad magic. But part of it's a fairy tale. I make a
lousy prince, but I have to try.

Funny, when you read this you'll know I didn't make it;
but here it is: MUSKY LAKE. Third, fifth, fourth. 247.

Cute, huh?

Now it's up to you. I'm going to put this in a place that
will remind you what he's turned into, what he did to this
poor kid, and left him here for us to find. I'll give it to him
to pass to you.

Good luck.

4

"It's in Wisconsin, a few miles out of a little place called
Oatavie," I said. "A lake, about half a mile across, in a high
valley with pine woods backing up the slopes all around. The
name on the map was Otter Lake, but I always thought of it
as Musky Lake. That's where I caught my first one."

Jess looked blank.

"A fish, a big one; a fighter. I took him on a ten-pound fly
line. It's a thing you don't forget."

"That area is heavily wooded, a desolation," Jess said. "Why
would he send you there?"

"I guess that's what we have to find out," I said, and stopped,
listening for a sound off to the left, back in what had been a
freight-loading bay—or maybe I just smelled something wrong.
I grabbed Jess's shoulder and just had time to say "Douse the
light" before there was a smash of sound and a blue-white
glare lit up the room like an operating theater and men in
black were coming through double doors that were swung
back wide from the old freight platform. We froze, watching
them fan out along both walls.

The spot we stood in was still in deep shadow that narrowed
in on us as a big dolly-mounted light came through the doors.
I ducked, felt over the floor, came up with a ragged piece of

steel plate the size of my hand. There was a nice zone of
shadow cast by a column that widened out in the direction
of the gallery. I threw the piece of plate high and hard, right
down the strip of shadow. It made a hell of a clatter when it
hit. The light swung off-side and we ducked out and ran for it.

Jess took the lead. He reached the brick wall and went flat
against and had his gun out, firing. I took the door in a running dive, and something boomed in the room behind me, and
Jess came through and fell against me and we went down together. Blood was pumping from a wound in his back I
couldn't have covered with my hand. I hooked his arm and he
was on his feet; his legs were like broken straws, but his knife
was in his hand.

"Leave me . . ." he sucked in air and it bubbled. ". . . by the
door . . . I'll greet . . . the first one . . . through . . ."

I slung him over my shoulder and ran. It was a fifty-foot
straightaway; I made it to the far end and got the door to the
receptionist's room open and a gun roared behind me and
slugs kicked chunks out of the frame. The only light was a faint
glow like moonlight from the ceiling strips. I crossed the room
in three jumps and my foot hit something under the dust layer
and I went down with Jess on top of me. I grabbed for him and
my hand slipped on blood that covered his left side. Big feet
were pounding close. I grabbed Jess by the belt and pitched
him into the office behind me, dived after him. Maybe my feet
cleared the door before the Blackie slammed into the room.

For a second or two there was a silence like the one just
after you pull the grenade pin. Then a heavy gun racketed
outside the door, one of those high-speed jobs that sprays out
slugs like a fire hose. The back of the door over me blew off in a
hail of plastic splinters. I hugged the floor and heard him come
across and I set myself and the door banged and he was
through, bringing the gun around, and I grabbed his ankle;
he arced backward and fell across Jess, kicking like a bass
hooked in the eye. I caught his gun before it hit the floor and

swung to see Jess's grin fade and his face set; and the knife in his hand fell in the dust, with Blackie blood on the blade.

I backed through the outer office trying to look two ways at once, and heard a soft sound and got the gun around in time and blew the face off a Blackie coming in from the hall. I got in the doorway, and put another burst out through it and went flat and somebody chewed up the door frame above my head. I could see the door Jess and I had come in by, half an hour before, standing an inch ajar, ten feet along the hall. Maybe they hadn't seen it yet in the bad light. If I was going to use it, it had to be now, before the place got crowded again. I came up and out and swung the gun and got off part of a burst before the Blackie who had been waiting for me blew the gun out of my hands. The impact of the slugs knocked me back against the wall. I saw blood on my sleeve, and I could tell I'd been hit in the body, but there was no pain, just a numbness spreading from the left side of my belly. I wedged myself against the door frame and watched him come across to me. He swung the gun over his shoulder by the strap and reached for me and I slid a hand in under the wrist and grabbed him and brought him in close and turned him and locked my forearm across his throat and broke up everything in there. I threw him away from me and waded across to the open panel and through it and got it closed behind me. For a few minutes, I leaned against the wall trying to talk myself out of lying down on the floor and having a nice long rest. I watched the blood flowing down the leg of the black scuba suit through a blackish haze full of little lights. There was some muffled noise racketing near me, but it didn't seem to concern me any more . . .

. . . I was lying down after all, and there was a lot of pounding going on, about six inches from my head. I felt like I ought to be on my feet, going somewhere, and I got up on all fours and discovered an anvil was chained to my left side. I fumbled with the place where the hook was in for a couple of minutes and then decided it was too much trouble. I moved and the anvil dragged and the hook cut into me and I was on my face again, resting.

OK, Dravek; show your stuff. Jess looked pretty good back there. Full of surprises, Jess was. Blackies will find that cute door pretty soon. Must be a nice trail leading to it. Shame to make it too easy for the mothering worms. Jess used to say that. Some Jess. Knew what he was getting into. A swimmer, Jess was. Better to go that way than here. In the dust. Helpful, at that. Caked up on my belly, along the arm. Not losing as much blood now. Blood Jess gave me. Nice place he had, good bed to lie in. Like to be there now . . .

I had four legs and four arms—or was it six of each? Tricky, figuring which ones to use when. Used to wonder if a horse didn't ever get mixed up, kick himself in the ankle. Four arms, and two legs, or maybe three. Wires all crossed, hard to make 'em work right. Missed then, hurt my face. *My God, but the pain is there now, Steve-boy. Help keep you awake, your mind on your business. Left, right, use the leg, drag the other one, keep going . . .*

CHAPTER SIX

I could hear the big generator pulling hard, and the sparks fountained out, and Frazier was yelling, but I couldn't hear what he was saying. I was watching the two-inch strip of cherry red weld stitching another plate into what was going to be a million-dollar setup. Million, hell, a hundred million, over the next ten years! Nobody could match Frazier when it came to tech management; he had a nose for that kind of talent that could comb a potential genius out of a crowd of downy-cheeked grads quicker than I could spot a shaved ace in a set of bicycles. The new process was going to turn the food-processing racket on its ear, and Draco, Inc. would be sole proprietor . . .

Frazier was there, hauling at my arm and pointing across the room. The outer door was open, a white glare against the dark, and I could see them silhouetted in it for a second before it closed behind them, her tall and slim, and the little one beside her. They were coming down into the big room and I waved and started that way and something up above shifted and sparks hissed and somebody yelled and the garish flicker of the big welding torch cut out. Frazier waved his arms and went over that way, fast. Somebody was yelling: ". . . it's hot! Get that plate clear, Brownie! Nulty, shut her down! All the way down!"

I got over to where a section of plate had dropped and sliced into the big cables ten feet from the side of the welder. There was a lot of smoke and a stench like burned cork. I got a couple of choice phrases ready for the framer who'd let it happen, and something made me turn and she was there, right in the thick of the smoke, holding something up in her hand, and I yelled and started toward her and saw her turn toward the sound of my voice and . . .

I was on the floor with my face against cold stone and I could still feel the scream that had ripped the inside out of my throat, and the churn of the generator was a deep throbbing coming through the floor and I got my head up and was looking at the open mouth of a manhole. There was a black toolcase lying beside it. It was Jess's. He'd left it there, after he'd used it to unlock the outer door. I was in the maintenance room above the big duct, and the rumbling noise was the pumps down below. I didn't remember how I'd gotten there.

I made a move to sit up and a big hook I'd forgotten about came down and ripped into my belly. I curled over it and rode the current of fire for a while; then I got a hand on the edge of the manhole and pulled. The fire was still burning, but I knew how to put it out. Down below the water was cold and black, deep enough to drown all the pain of living.

My face was over the opening; I could see a black glint down below. *One more pull, Dravek; you can do it.* One arm wasn't helping much, but who needs two arms? I used the good knee and felt my chest go over the edge and I was sliding down and then falling into soft black that closed over me . . .

2

The shock brought me out of it. For a while—maybe a few seconds, maybe longer—I rolled with the turbulence. Then I slammed something hard and the pain went clear through me from the top of my head to the end of my toes; and all of a sudden I knew I was in the duct, being carried along by the high-pressure stream, with my head banging the walls at regular intervals. I felt the duct widen, and I remembered the louvers ahead and got a hand on the water jets and pointed myself upstream and gave them a blast. I slammed the louvers hard, hung up there for a second or two—then slid between them and was out in the deep river, rolling end over end.

The cold was cutting through the suit, and I groped a little and thumbed the heat control up some, but not too much, because a little low-temperature anesthesia was a good idea for right then.

While I was doing all this, the river was taking me along to wherever it was going, which even in this day of improved methods for propagating human misery was probably the sea. I've been a sailor, but I never liked the idea of Davy Jones's locker. I got my head pointed upstream again and used my jets and steered for the right side of the channel. It wasn't easy to maneuver, because one leg seemed to be dead from the hip down, and the left arm had something wrong with it. The fire in my belly didn't seem important right then. I figured I'd get to think about it plenty, later, if there was a later.

I used the jets and edged forward and in less than a minute found an iron rung and held on. I had one good leg and about an arm and a half; the fingers on the left one didn't seem to want to close like they should. I got an overhead grip and pulled up and got a toe on a rung and made another foot. This went on for a long time. Two or three times I forgot what I was doing and started to slide back, but each time an instinct that used to keep monkeys from falling out of trees made my hand grab and hold on.

The time came when I reached and there wasn't any rung, or any wall, and that seemed like a dirty shame and I went on feeling the air for about as long as it takes to light a slow fire under a missionary and watch it burn down. After a while I got a grip with a fingernail and hauled the legs up over the edge, which was no harder than swinging a piano in my teeth, and fell a couple of feet. That put me where I'd been trying to get: on my back in an empty street, with four slugs in me and cops looking for me, wanting to finish the job.

I crawled over to the nearest wall and lay against it and tried to check myself over. The trouble with the arm seemed to be due to a hole I could stick the end of my little finger in, just below the elbow. The leg was a little more complicated. The hip was broken up, but there was no wound on the outside; the suit was intact there. That meant the slug had gone in through the belly and hit the pelvic bone from the inside.

That brought me to the big one. I got my hand inside the suit just far enough to feel what I knew was there, and passed out cold.

When I came out of that one, I was lying on my side kissing cold pavement and watching someone ducking along in the shadows cast by a light on a tall pole far up the street. I thought about reaching for the the little gadget Jess had told me was a reliable short-range killer, but nothing happened. I was part of the stone; just an eye peering back from that last thin edge, watching the show.

The oncoming figure went into a shadow that was too black to see through and came out, closer, and skittered across the street to my side and came along to me and stopped and looked both ways before she looked down. It was Minka, the girl with the blue hair. I started to open my mouth to give her my usual cheery greeting, and her face swelled up and spread until it blanked out the light and I gave it all up and let the darkness take me.

3

Voices were talking.

". . . say this cull's a Blackie-twister! That makes him fast freight!"

"Don't be hasty. It's a prime hulk. This is no Dirtie. He'll fetch top price from a Forkwaters stiff-hack, once he's patched a little—"

"The insides are messed up bad, Darklord. It wouldn't be worth the expense to rebuild—"

"I said *patch*, Acey! Caveat empty, as the old saying goes. If he's moved quickly, who's to know?"

"I say slice him. The heart alone—"

"Have you no sense of the fitness of things? Look at that skin! As white and smooth as a star-lady's rump." A meaty chuckle. "And I speak from first hand . . ." The chuckle went out of the voice and a hard note came in. "But where's his cull-mark, eh? Mmmmm? He must have his tattoo; he must have. He must. He . . ."

"Too much talk! Talk makes trouble. Cut 'em pretty and they'll fetch enough. Don't get greedy, that's the secret. Don't get greedy and don't listen to talk. He's no trimmed Cruster on a drop. There's something chancey about this weed. I say slice him, slice him fine!"

"Seems a pity, with wholemeat units bringing what they do; but perhaps you're right. Very well, Acey; limb and gut, I think, and of course, epidermal—but cut it nicely, no telltales—"

Then I heard a new voice, one I'd heard before, somewhere.

". . . that filthy little slicer touch him!"

"My dear, you do Acey a disservice! He's the finest technician in the business, ETORP-trained, mind you! If it hadn't been for a trifling indiscretion in certain informal arrangements . . ."

"Where's Jess?"

"Who knows? We found only this one—what they left of him."

"Did he talk?"

"My dear, he was fully occupied with surviving."

"I want him fixed! You know I can pay!"

"Ah, but will you pay in negotiable coin?"

"Just fix him!"

"Ah, Minky-pet, grudging affection is cold comfort to a tenderhearted man like myself, hardly worth the bartering for . . ." Heavy breathing. "Well, Minky-love. And after you've been so precious formal with good Uncle Abdullah . . ."

"Do something for him! Can't you see he's bleeding to death?"

"Patience, love. This hulk is in pitiable condition. It requires expensive internals. The liver is a ruin; two of those nasty little darts have shredded it into sausage! Now where am I to find a sound liver on such notice? Such organs don't grow on trees—"

"Lucky for you they grow on men. You've got plenty of those."

"You'd have me slice one of my own, for the benefit of this stranger?"

"No. For the benefit of your own greasy flesh!"

"Hmmm. Frankly, and most directly put. As it happens, I have a fine fresh liver on hand, just gutted out, a trifle large for the trade, but this big fellow shouldn't mind that."

"Give him whatever he needs. Just fix him, I don't care how you do it!"

There was more talk after that, but I wasn't paying much attention—the pain was rising around me like pouring day at a brass foundry. I heard some small, whimpery sounds, figured out they were coming from me, tried to cut them out, gave up, and groaned out loud. Somebody was hauling at my arm, somebody was sawing off my leg. It didn't seem to matter much. I was off somewhere in the rosy distance now, floating on a nice soft cloud with just a few needles in it that poked me when I tried to move. Somebody came along with a skinning knife then, and cut me into slices and stretched them out in the sun to dry, and somebody else collected the slices and sewed them back together, swearing all the while. It didn't interest me a lot; but after a while the voices got louder, more insistent, and I opened my mouth to tell them to go away and then there was a thick smell like all the hospital corridors I ever smelled dumped in my face at once and the cloud faded into a thin mist that closed over me and shut out the light and the sound and I spun back down into nothingness.

CHAPTER SEVEN

I woke up propped in a bed, blinking across at a room lit like the seduction scene from *Don Giovanni*. There was a lot of flowery gauze curtain, pale yellow velvet drapes pulled back from floor-to-ceiling glass, a tangerine rug, a couple of small paintings that were swirls of pink and orange and burnt umber, a few sticks of furniture that looked as if they would disappear if you pushed the right button.

Minka was sitting in one of the chairs. She looked better minus the orange paint and the blue hair and the ribbons. There was a filmy toga-like wrap around her now, that showed off her figure better than a shower bath. Her hair was a soft brown, and her mouth looked soft and young without the paint. I opened my mouth to say hello and a grunt came out. She looked up.

"How is it?" Her voice was soft, like somebody who's been there herself.

"A little confused," I said. "But resting comfortably." It came out in a weak chirp, like a baby bird. I had to lie back and rest up after the effort.

She was standing by the bed. "Jess?" she said.

"Dead."

"I guess I knew; but they said you couldn't have come that far alone, with all those spinners in you."

I had a sudden thought and moved a hand down, not without a certain effort, and felt a leg where a leg ought to be.

"You're all right now," she said. "That little man with the rat's eyes is a wizard."

"I seem to remember something about needing some replacement parts."

"He grafted a liver, and some nerve tissue, and the femoral artery was in bad shape. It was luck he had stock on hand. There was a man, a giant, who'd been killed just a few hours before."

I let that one hang in the air. She went away then, and I had another nice nap. I woke up hungry, and she fed me soup. I ate it and watched her face. She was a girl with lots on her mind.

When the soup was gone, she made a lot out of fluffing pillows and getting the light just right. Then she lit up a dope stick and said, "Why did you do it?"

"There was some information I wanted. I had an idea I might find it there."

"And did you?"

"I'm not sure."

"Jess thought you knew something that was very important for—certain people."

"He was wrong about that."

"Who are you? Where did you come from?" She sounded as if she hated to ask the question and didn't want to know the answer.

"This is going to sound a little screwy," I said. "But I'm not sure about that either."

"You mean—amnesia?"

"Maybe that's what you'd call it. I know my name, and I can tie my own shoes. Outside of that . . ."

"Jess said he found you in the park. He said a cutter squad

attacked you and you . . . killed them with your bare hands."

"That's where it starts. Before that it's a little mixed up. I thought I had a few clues, but I seem to be two other guys."

"You're a strange man. You have a strange way of talking—and not only the accent. You joke about death and suffering."

"I was hoping maybe you could tell me something useful on those subjects."

"What do you mean?"

"About some of the funny angles of all this. About why Jess thought I was important enough to bring home for a souvenir, and why the cops are after me."

"I know what he told me," she said. "That's all. About the rest—I don't know anything."

"You must have a few ideas. You paid the fat man's price."

She looked at me and a shudder took her and shook her like a dog shakes a rat.

"I'm sorry," I said. "We're a cagey pair, sparring around and trying to sneak a look at the other fellow's hand. Why don't we try it showdown?"

"I've told you all I can." She looked past me. Her face was tight.

"Sure," I said. "In that case maybe I'd better catch another few winks. We wouldn't want all that fine craftsmanship to go to waste."

2

I did a lot of sleeping during the next few days. It might have been something the girl put in my soup—or maybe it was just Mother Nature, stitching me back together. There were a lot of things I didn't care for in the Twenty-second Century, but their medicine was as far ahead of the old familiar GP as a 707 was a dog cart. Minka stayed close, doing nurse's chores with a lot of efficiency and as little conversation as possible. Quite a few days slipped by, while I lay on my back and watched the clouds out beyond a balcony like Jess's and didn't think about a lot of things. Then one evening I had a sudden urge to get out of bed and sample some fresh air.

I got a leg over the side of the bed and that worked OK so I stood up and started across toward the columns. I was half-way there when Minka came into the room.

"What are you doing?" She was right there, with an arm around me, propping me up. "Are you trying to kill yourself?"

Her hand was against my bare back; it was smooth and soft and warm. The arm that went with it was nice, too. I put an arm around her, pulled her to me.

"Are you out of your mind . . . ?" She whispered. But she didn't pull away. Up close like this I could smell the faint per-fume of her hair. My hands were on the slimness of her waist, and I moved them down over the curve of hips that were the way hips ought to be. The tissue paper thing she was wearing got in my way and I threw it into the corner. Then her arms were around my neck, and her body was against mine, and her skin was like the finest silk ever spun, and her lips were as soft as a whisper in the dark.

"Steve," she said in my ear. "Oh, Steve . . ."

3

"You're a strange, savage man," Minka said. She was lying on her side on the bed looking at me, and the moonlight from the terrace reflected in her eyes and made pale highlights in her hair. "I've never known a man like you, Steve."

"You don't know me now," I said. "I don't know myself."

"I brought you here because I wanted to learn things from you. But I don't care about that, now."

"I've got to go, Minka. You know that."

"Stay here, Steve. You'll be safe here. Out there they'll kill you."

"Out there is where the answers are."

"Jess wanted answers—and they killed him. Why not forget all that—"

"There are places I've got to go, things that want me to do them."

"Things that are more important than what we might have together?" In the pale light her body glowed like ivory.

"You're all the woman a man could want," I said. "But this is something I have to do."

"Why? Do you think you can change the world, like Jess did? You can't, Steve. No one man can. We've made this world what it is. It's the way we wanted it: safe, comfortable, plenty of food for all, plenty of leisure, a long life—for those who don't rock the boat. You've been dirtside; you've seen how they live there. Do you want to go back to that?"

"I'm no world-saver, Minka. But I don't like unfinished business."

"They've lost your trail; they'll never find you! I can get you a new tag, a cullmark—everything—"

I shook my head.

"Why are you doing this? What could you possibly learn that would be worth risking your life for?"

"It's something I have to do for a friend. He's counting on me."

She laughed, not a pretty laugh. "And you wouldn't be the one to let a friend down, would you, Steve?"

4

I left the next afternoon, briefed to the ears, armed with a neat little watch-pocket blaster, and feeling better than anybody had a right to, two weeks after having new insides installed. I rode an elevator that dropped so fast my stomach was ready to climb out and have a look by the time the door opened and palmed me out onto a pavement halfway between a street and a corridor. A cold light like a winter afternoon was filtering down from a high glass roof. There were lots of people, pushing along on important business; the grim looks on their faces were normal, but the clothes they wore were like something from Westercon II. A tired-looking fellow in bulbous, color-slashed bloomers pushed past me using his elbow like an experienced commuter. A fellow in baggy-kneed tights and floppy sleeves jostled a woman in pink ruffs out of his way; she passed it on to a young kid in a tight coverall with dummy laces at the wrists and shins. Nobody looked at me. I felt like I was back home.

I moved off along the walk, mingled with men in capes and three-cornered hats, women in all-over ruffles and stand-up lace collars and some stripped to the waist and painted like barber poles, and a few of both sexes wrapped in old bedsheets. They looked like survivors of a three-day fancy-dress ball.

There were signs plastered over the walls in screaming pink and electroshock blue and agony yellow. I picked one that read DRINK in purple script and turned in at what seemed to be an open doorway, but something banged me on the nose like a glass wall, and something else went *bzzapp!* and I was back out on the pavement. To hell with it. I didn't need a drink anyway.

Up ahead, there was a big TV screen ten feet square sticking out over the walk, with words and pictures flickering across it. Letters across the top said "THRVEE MALL WESTOFCL." I watched it for a minute while quick flashes of strange faces and factory smokestacks and desert landscapes and explosions came and went over subtitles in condensed headline prose.

A little farther along I came to what Minka had told me to look for: A wide frosted-glass front over blank doors with cryptic signs that said things like "PVR SLD II (9)" and "OUT—Z99-over."

I went through one of the doors and was in a narrow chute like the bull comes out of, with a turnstile blocking it. There was a slot at one side about the right size for a silver dollar, but I didn't have a silver dollar. I leaned on it and it leaned back. There was nobody around to ask questions of, even if I'd been in a mood to attract attention that way. I braced a foot against the crossbar and tried again. Something inside made little tinkly sounds and it spun free.

Ten feet beyond it, the passage right-angled and I was looking at a blank screen dazzling with little points of light. There were a lot of buttons beside it. I pushed a couple of them, as instructed, and said: "Routing for West Bore."

The screen blipped red and white and blanked. So much for the kind of cooperation I get out of inanimate objects. I opened my mouth to ask the question again, louder, and something clacked behind me and I did a fast turn and a female came out of a doorway. She had a hard, good-looking face with no paint except a green dot on her right cheek and dull silver on her lips. Her figure looked good enough, what I could see of it under a gray coverall.

"Passengers are restricted—" she started her pitch.

"I'll bet they are, gorgeous," I cut it off. "I asked it a question and it gave me a smart answer. Maybe you can do better." Her expression slid sideways a little, not quite as cocky now, but ready to be, as soon as she got the lie of the land. "The entry monitor indicates an all-categories tag," she said in a tone that had shifted a couple of points toward civil. That would be a reference to the sounds of breaking metal that had come out of the turnstile when I leaned on it.

"Right," I gave her a significant look. "You know what that means."

She didn't meet my eye. "You're with the Commission?" she tried to sound brisk but there was just a hint of a quaver in her voice.

"Would I be here if I wasn't?"

"If I may record your credentials—as a matter of routine—"

"We're dispensing with the routine, Miss—what was that name?"

"Gerda. I. L. Gerda, nine-three, Second, provisional."

"All right, Gerda, let's not waste the Commission's time."

"If you'll give me your authority reference—"

"This is hush-hush," I said. "Off the record. If it wasn't I wouldn't need you, would I, Gerda?" I sweetened it with the sort of smile her turnkey personality seemed to call for.

She twitched a couple of cheek muscles at me and said, "If you'll come this way . . ."

I followed a nice hip action along the corridor to an iron gate, and about then I noticed a bell dinging somewhere in the distance.

"What is it, Gerda, a cross?" I grabbed her arm and she tried to kick me. She was looking mean enough to bite, now.

"You entered on a forged tag," she'd gone shrill on me. "Don't try to leave!" I pushed her out of the way and she went for my eyes, and I slapped her, hard. Her nose started to bleed. Something clanged back of the grill and a red light went on. Another bell racketed, nearby.

"Don't dare leave here," Miss Gerda squalled. "You're under criminal arrest!"

"Sorry," I said. "As it happens, I'm late for a Ping-pong date at the YW. Better open it, Gerda."

Her eyes hated me, but she pushed the right spot and the gate snapped back. There was a sound from back the way I'd come and the girl twisted and threw herself down and something went *ssstt!* and a gnat's wing brushed my cheek and kicked a chip out of the wall. I got a quick flash of two men in tight black coming through the door twenty yards back along the passage. I cleared the gate just as a second shot whanged off it, kicked it shut, and ran like hell.

5

An hour and a half of fast travel later I stepped out into a concourse crowded with people looking like travelers have looked ever since home got to be a place to get away from. I saw a few lads in dark uniforms standing here and there eyeballing the scene, but the uniforms were gray and had MVNT

CNTRL lettered on their pocket patches. But they packed guns, just like real Blackies.

There was a railing on the right, and below it a spread of pavement with a rank of big torpedoes lit up like Christmas trees. Little cars like U-dodge-ems were ducking around between them, ferrying passengers. I went along the gallery, took the down escalator. Two of the men in gray were standing at the bottom looking at faces; two pairs of eyes lit on me. I felt them all the way down and across the tarmac, but it must have just been my conscience bothering me. They let me go.

I crossed the big glassed-in concourse full of people and flashing lights and noise, went down a sloping ramp and was outside, under open sky. There weren't many people here. In the distance, the city lights were a jeweled wall.

The signs here weren't much help. Over on the left, beyond half a dozen sets of what could have been roller-coaster rails, something whooshed and a low-slung vehicle riding on two fore-and-aft-mounted wheels came slamming down the track and stopped and the lid popped up and a fat man and a thin woman got in. It racketed off and another one came down the line and curbed itself.

There was a low rail between me and the cars. I jumped it, went along a narrow strip that looked as if it might not electrocute me; I went around the back of the car and put a hand on the door and behind me a cool voice said, "Stop there."

I turned around, not too fast. Two gray uniforms were coming over, relaxed, taking their time. One of them said, "Movement Control," and the other one said, "Step over here." No pleases and thank-you's for these boys.

I came around the car and across in the indicated direction. The one on the left went past me toward the car, which put me between them and a yard from his partner. I doubled my fist and hit him low in the stomach and grabbed the front of the gray blouse and swung him around. The other one had heard something; he came around, reaching for his hip. I threw his friend at him and socked him in the throat and vaulted into the car and slapped the big red button and the wheels screamed and I was off.

CHAPTER EIGHT

For the first hour I drove with my shoulders tight, listening for the sirens or whatever they might have thought up to replace them in this new, improved-model world. Then I had a thought that cheered me some. This was an Autopike; the coppers probably had ways of pinpointing any vehicle operating on it anywhere—as long as he was locked into the system. But I was on manual. As long as I stayed with the pack, there was no way to pick me out—maybe.

I held the car at 200 mph for five hours. About a hundred miles northwest of where the little map unrolling on the dash screen said the sprawl of light called Chago was, I pulled off on a lay-by marked with big arrows of luminous rose paint. Inside my left jacket cuff there was a plastic button Minka had put there to fool the scanners. I ripped it loose and tossed it on the floor. Then I flipped the controls to AUTO and hopped out. The car jumped off from the rail and curveted on her two wheels along the metal strip in the road, angled out, and joined the main lane, picking up speed fast, running empty. She went over the rise howling, with her controls pegged at top emergency speed. I went over the guard rail and got a grip on the edge and felt for a toehold and started down.

2

By the time the sun was an hour in the sky, I was five miles north of the pike, working my way through a swampy patch toward the higher ground north and west of me. The years had made a lot of difference in what had been farming country and tame woods back in my hunting days. Now it had the look of the forest primeval. The oaks and elms and maples were four feet across at the base, and there was a new tree I'd never seen before, a tapered, smooth-barked conifer that probably all started from a salted nut dropped by a tourist along the roadside. It was late in the year, later than the temperature would make you think. Leaves were already turning red, and the smell of fall was in the air.

This part of the route was easy; I steered by the sun, stayed away from the right-of-way of the few roads I came to that had cars on them. It seemed that the national passion for touring the country in the family station wagon had finally worked itself out. People either stayed in their hives, close to the buttons they needed to push for life's necessities, or did their traveling by air or cross-country tube. I saw a few high contrails, and once a copter whiffled past a mile away at treetop level; but whatever the boys used to sniff out fugitives wasn't geared to a guy without the little telltale set in the bone back of the ear. I was an untagged man, and as invisible to them as an Indian was to General Braddock.

Just before noon I crossed a strip of broken concrete with a rusted sign fallen on its face that seemed to say US 30 A. As well as I could remember the map, that would put me somewhere to the east of Rockford. I had a full set of blisters, but otherwise was holding up swell. The leg gave me a little trouble, but Minka had told me that I was walking on the best permanent-oiled titanium alloy hip joint money could buy, so I let that thought console me.

Late in the afternoon a pair of copters came pretty close, crisscrossing the country to the north. They seemed to have a general idea where I was, and that worried me some; but maybe it was just coincidence. They worked their way on to the east and I had the world to myself again.

Just before sunset I came up onto a cleared stretch covered with concrete foundations and broken-down chimneys and a few walls still standing, well blacked by a fire. Letters cut into a piece of cornice from what would have been the town's best building said BRODHEAD NATIONAL BANK. That put me over the line into Wisconsin, about thirty miles south of where I wanted to be.

I spent the night there, on the back porch of a brick house at the north edge of town. It wasn't that it was more comfortable than a nest in the woods, but maybe by then I was getting a little lonely. And even in ruins, the little town was something that was almost familiar.

I went on before the sun was up, hit a little stream west of the town, followed it northwest. About noon I saw an airplane, a short-coupled job with vertical jets that made a big noise and curled leaves in the tops of the trees. It went past, a quarter of a mile north of me, moving slow enough to make me stand under a tree and pretend to be a natural formation. A few minutes later, I crossed another road trace and was into rising ground. I picked a route along a ravine between wooded ridges and in the next hour hit the dirt three times when little one-seater aircraft came whistling over at low altitude. It began to look as if the Blackies were closing in on me. How, I didn't know. There didn't seem to be any posses combing the underbrush with dogs so far; that was something. I went on, keeping to cover now. But I was starting to feel hemmed in.

By midafternoon I had crossed three ridges and was coming down into a valley that had a half-familiar look. The trees were a hundred years bigger than they should have been, but otherwise it all looked just the way it had the last time.

I couldn't exactly place the last time.

I went on down to a gravel strip that had been a road, thought it over and tried the left-hand direction and ten minutes later recognized the turn-off that led up to Musky Lake.

Things got a little more rugged after that. Twilight was coming on, and it was chilly up here on the high ground. There was a lot of loose shale that made the footing tricky, and the light was no help. It took me an hour to reach the top of the ridge. The growth was heavy here. I picked a route back toward where the road sliced through and saw a light through the trees and hit the dirt. It seemed that Musky Lake wasn't the unspoiled wilderness it was in the old days, after all.

I counted the lights shining through the dusk. There were eight of them, spaced at regular intervals on the other side of the rise of ground ahead. I was still admiring this view when something big and dark with lots of blue and red navigation lights whiffled overhead and disappeared over the ridge. The place I was heading for seemed to be a popular spot with the airborne set—and the look of the jobs I'd seen spelled military.

In front of me, a deep black shadow angled across my route, the same gully that I'd bridged once with a pine log. The log was gone, and I had to go down through a healthy growth of brambles to get across it, but up ahead was the ridge, and on the other side of it was the spot I was aiming at. I made it in another five minutes and pushed my face out between broken rock to take my first look at what had been the prettiest spot this side of Wales, with the lake in the center like a star sapphire laid out on green velvet.

It wasn't like that now. In the late twilight I could see trees that thinned out for fifty feet down the rocky slope to a stretch of open ground a hundred feet wide and a cluster of buildings beyond, all of it lit like a prison yard on hanging night.

3

It was full dark now, with no moon. A couple more copters had flitted overhead, and a big VTOL job had made a noisy descent a couple of miles away, on the other side of the valley.

I backed off below the ridge line and started around. An hour later I was on the east side of the valley, looking up at a tall building with lots of windows with lights behind them, and fenced grounds all around. The rest of the enclosure seemed to be nothing but virgin forest. Somebody had gone to a lot of trouble to wall in a patch of woods no different than the seventy miles of the same thing I'd traveled through for a day and two nights getting here. Maybe the place had been converted into a private resort for the big shots of this day and age. The big building would be the ritzy hotel, and the block-houses over on the other side were the servants' quarters. And the air traffic wasn't looking for me; they were ferrying the rich tourists in to enjoy a rustic week-end back of a wall that kept the peasants out.

It was a swell theory, but I still kept my head down and looked for the angle.

It took me half an hour to find a route in the dark. The old drainage ditch, choked level with weeds, was it. It wasn't over two feet deep where it went between the lights. I hugged the dirt and did it with my fingers and toes, an inch at a time. Fifteen minutes of this put me far enough inside the lights to risk sticking my head up. The coast was clear. I moved off in the cover of some deep grass to take a closer look at the big building.

4

An eight-foot fence made of black iron spears with big barbed heads was only the first obstacle. Beyond the bars a sweep of manicured lawn broke like green surf against a line of tailored shrubbery, and back of every clump a light was placed just right to cover a section of the perimeter. There were Blackies here—squads of them, pacing around the grounds like a bunch of butlers looking for the duchess's lost diamond choker. They had packs clipped to their belts with wires lead-ing to the sides of their helmets, and I didn't need a set of technical specs to tell that these were something that worked a lot better than leashed bloodhounds. I stepped on a dry stick about then and two of the boys turned and started drifting my way. I backed out softer-footed than the time I stumbled into a cave that had a sleeping cougar in it, and moved back a couple of hundred yards into deep woods.

It took me an hour to scout all the way around the fence. It enclosed about fifty acres of park with the fairy palace in the middle and a nice little pad for short take-off aircraft at one side, well stocked with everything from one-man hoppers to a deep-bellied heavyweight big enough to carry a full battalion complete with artillery. Nothing I saw gave me any encouragement.

About then I noticed some activity over on the left, not far from where I'd made my first approach. A section of fence swung out and a small air-cushion car came through it and moved along in a puddle of yellow-white made by its bow and stern lights and the gate closed again. There was nothing in that for me.

The car came along my way, and I faded back along a sort of trail until it dawned on me it was using the same trail. I did a fade into the brush then, and lay flat with my cheek in the dirt while it whirled its dirt cloud past and snorted on off toward the barracks across the valley.

I stayed there for a while and told myself I was watching the lights moving beyond the fence. After a while my chin bumped the ground and woke me up. I got up and moved back deeper into the woods, with a vague kind of idea of finding a nice dark spot to hole up in and nap until the next brain wave hit me.

The going was easier in among the big timber. There was a slight downward drift to the ground, and not much in the way of underbrush. Then I saw a gleam ahead that looked like riffled water with moonlight on it and came down the last slope and clear of the trees and was looking at Musky Lake.

5

For a long, timeless minute I looked out across the water and listened to the old voices, whispering to me over all the years, as if no time had passed at all. From here, you couldn't see the barracks or the fenced-in tower; just the lake, stretching to the far shore with the rising wall of big pines behind it, and over to the left the point where the cabin had stood, the one Frazier and I built barehanded one summer just after the war. I looked toward it and at first the shadows there under the big trees fooled me, and then I blinked hard and was still seeing the same thing. The cabin was still standing, right where we'd left it.

I took the path along the soft ground at the edge of the water, and had the feeling that if I blinked again, it would go away. I came up on it from the left, the way we used to come down from shooting in the woods, and even the melon patch was still there, a little overgrown, but clear enough in the moonlight. The dock was off to the right, and the old flat-bottomed skiff was tied up at the end of it, with the bow off-shore, the way I'd always anchored her. I had the damnedest impulse to yell and see if Frazier would come out the door, waving a jug and telling me to hurry up, the serious drinking was about to begin . . .

I came up with the little gun in my hand, skirted the place at a hundred yards, then worked my way in, ready to drop or shoot first, whichever way it worked out. Fifty feet from the cabin I lay flat and watched the back windows. Fifteen minutes went by, with nothing but a few mosquitos whining around my head to prove I wasn't a ghost. Part of that shrewd calculating machine that was what passed for the Dravek intelligence was telling me I was taking chances, wasting time leafing through the faded gardenias of my yesterdays; but another part didn't give a damn. This was a place I knew, that was part of my life, the life I remembered. From here, strange people like Jess and strange places like the slum they called dirtside and man-eating corporations called ETORP seemed like something you'd think up in the dark hours of the night after too much lobster and fruitcake.

I made my final approach standing up. If anybody had the place staked out they could nail me as well creeping as walking, as long as I was coming their way. But nobody jumped out and put a spotlight in my eyes. I came around the side of the cabin and heard a bullfrog say moo, like a cow, down by the water. There was a small window to the left of the door. I came up to it and looked in, saw nothing but some reflected moonlight, went on past it to the door. It opened without an argument. The hinges squeaked; they always squeaked.

Inside nothing had changed, not even the dust on the floor or the soot on the ceiling above the fireplace. I tucked my toy gun away and started in to search the place.

CHAPTER NINE

An hour later the sky was beginning to gray up and I had covered the one-room cabin three times and turned up nothing.

I sat on the edge of the bunk and chewed my teeth and tried to be as smart as the note-writer expected me to be. He said as soon as I got here I'd know where to look.

The cabin was a lousy place to hide anything. The walls were plain one-inch ship-lapped redwood, with open studs, no paneling inside. The ceiling was bare rafters and boards. There was one cupboard, with a few chipped plates and cups in it. The fireplace had a liberal drift of ashes and a few chips of charred wood. The bathroom had nothing but what you'd expect, and the flush tank hadn't yielded any secrets suspended by a string from the float, or inside it. And if there were any compartments under the floor, they weren't anything I'd had a hand in. The trick drawer back of the strongbox in my office had been the extent of my instinct for conspiracy.

A little pale light was coming in past the red-and-white checked curtains that had been some short-term girl friend's idea of woodsy atmosphere. I went over to the door and eased it open and stepped out and looked out across the lake and just like that, I had it.

2

It was one of those days that stick in your mind down through the years; a hot day, with a breeze on the lake that riffled the surface just enough to bring the bass out of the deep hollows and up from under the sunken logs to snap at the big juicy flies the wind was bringing out over the water. Frazier and I had landed half a boat full before the wind died and they stopped hitting. The two girls—Gwen and Rosanne—had laid out a nice table while we cleaned the haul and packed what we couldn't eat in the freezer. After dinner we went down to the shore and sat under the trees and finished off the bottle—the third bottle of the day. We had a big laugh with it: the third fifth on the Fourth of July.

There'd been a big pine stump outside the cabin. We counted the rings; two hundred and forty-seven. Then we buried the dead soldier under it, with full military honors. . . .

3

It took me under ten minutes to find the stump, grub away enough packed leaves and hard dirt to find the gap down among the roots and pull out the bottle. The label was gone and the metal screw cap had been replaced with a hard, waxy plug, but it looked like the same bottle. I held it up to the light and made out something inside it, pale through the brown glass.

My mouth felt a little dry and my pulse was rocking my hand a little, but otherwise there was just the feeling of unnatural awareness you get when all the days of anticipation focus down to the second you've been working toward. I made a couple of tries to get the sealing wax loose, then cracked the neck off the bottle and reached in and teased the paper out.

It was just one sheet, folded and rolled, and all it had on it was two words:

COUGAR CAVE

4

It was a stiff half-hour's climb up through dense timber to the escarpment on the east side of the valley where the bare rock pushed up a hundred and fifty feet higher than it did anywhere else along the rim. There were boulders there as big as London buses, piled where the glacier had left them; and in among them there were a lot of cosy little caves where Frazier and I had flushed everything from weasels to a mothy brown bear. The one where I'd met the cougar was up high, with an approach across a rockface that made it too hard to get to to interest most critters, or most hunters. The time I'd gone up there I was chasing a wolverine with a 30-30 slug in him who didn't know when to lie down and be dead. It wasn't the kind of chore that was any fun; I did it because if I hadn't, a long line of hunting Draveks would have come out of their graves spinning like roulette wheels. I went up soft and easy and my carcajou was there, a yard inside the overhang, dead. I had one foot up to make the big mistake when I smelled cat and saw him, curled up in the back, logy after a kill maybe, just starting to move. I faded back and slid all the way to the bottom and spent the next week growing new skin on my palms and the seat of my pants. I'd never been back.

The sun was making rose-colored patterns up high on the rockface. I went up fast, not being any fonder of the climb than the last time, but even less fond of doing it in broad daylight. I made it to the ledge in ten minutes and came up over it and went flat, and looked back into shadows. It was no different than the last time, except for no kitty.

Inside, there was the same smell of wet rock and animal droppings that all these caves had. I had to duck to get in past the outer vestibule where the wolverine had died, and was in a bigger chamber, about right for garaging a VW, if you could get it inside. The floor here was the dirt that had drifted in during the last few thousand years, more or less smooth-packed; the walls slanted up to a craggy ceiling with air spaces with roots showing in them. That gave me enough light to show me that things were just like I left them, without a hiding place for anything bigger than an aspirin. If I was hoping to find a ten-volume journal telling me what it was all about, I was out of luck.

The trip in had taken forty minutes; the search consumed another thirty seconds. I prowled the cave again, used up that odd half minute. This was the end of the line. It had been a swell chase up to now, but it looked like I was going to go back to the frat house minus the motorman's glove after all.

I went back into the outer cave and looked out over a view of pine tops down to the sparkle of the lake a mile away and tried to think like a guy sitting in the dark beside a coffin writing notes to a stranger about something that he had to do that he knew was going to kill him; but all that got me was an attack of claustrophobia.

I looked over the anteroom, went out and studied the front porch and wondered how many little men with binoculars were watching me, went back in and scraped my foot across the spot where the devil cat had used up the last of his chips, and saw the shine of metal . . .

5

It was a stainless steel lock box, not locked; all it had in it was a heavy plastic envelope, sealed. I got that open and took out a sheet of paper with typing on it and read:

> In the back room. Look up high, on the left. The opening looks too small, but you can make it. About fifty feet.
> Brace yourself.

6

The hole was there all right, and it looked too small, just like the man said. But I got up there and got my shoulders in and twisted over on my side and started in.

The tunnel slanted down after the first couple of yards, tight going but just on the right side of possible. In a couple of places I felt smooth clay where somebody had done some excavating.

Twice I thought I'd been stopped, and had to back off and try again, at a new angle; and once I got my head through into a pocket my shoulders wouldn't pass and was stuck there for a minute, feeling the weight of a mountain crushing me flat before I worked an arm up and pushed a fallen stone out of the way and went on through.

It was pitch dark once I was below the broken rock level and into the solid stuff. This part of the tunnel was wider. I did it on my hands and knees, using my head for a bumper. Even in the dark I could tell this was a man-made shaft now. It dropped at a thirty-degree angle, after about twenty feet cut hard to the left, then left again and down another twenty feet, and there was light ahead.

I stopped there and felt of my gun for whatever good that did me and listened hard, trying to make up my mind whether I heard a faint sound coming from down below or not, decided it was just a ringing in my ears, and did the last few feet to another right-angle turn and was in a room.

It wasn't a cave. The walls were cut smooth and faced with concrete. The floor was natural stone, ground smooth. The ceiling was high enough that I didn't have to duck. The light was coming from a strip down the center of it that shed a pale green light on something bulky that almost filled the little room. It was a cylinder, ten feet long, five feet in diameter, looped and hung with plastic piping and wires. I'd seen something like it once before, in the sealed wing under my old plant. That one had had a corpse in it. This one felt different.

I came up to it easy, as if there might be something there that I didn't want to startle. I put a hand against the side of the big tank and felt a vibration so faint that if I hadn't been alone under forty feet of solid rock I wouldn't have thought it was there at all. The curve of the top of the thing was a little above my eye level, but there was a platform there for me to step up on. I did, and looked down at a clear plastic plate about a foot square, set in the top curve of the tank. It was misty, and I had to lean close to see through it and when I did a big hand as cold as death closed on my chest and squeezed.

The face behind the cloudy glass was that of a child, a little girl no more than six years old, pale and translucent as a china doll.

It was the face from the dreams.

7

I found the letter lying on the platform and got it open and by holding it three inches from my face I could read it:

She's here. Number Three was right; a billion dollars worth of security systems, but our route slides under all of it. Frazier built it when he was building the Keep, right under his nose. He knew him; too tough to know when he met a man that was tougher.

There's just one place more to go now. I think I've got a chance, maybe even a good chance; but I'm leaving what I've got for you, in case I slip. Maybe I was a little too tricky, feeding it to you in pieces, but it makes a broken trail that can't be cracked by an outside man with one lucky find. Except the one man, and I'm counting on the trick paint to take him out. What I planted in the box for him to find should make him happy enough to call off his dogs, at least long enough to give you your chance, if it comes to that. He knows I'm here, somewhere, and I don't

know how. He knows how I'd figure the play; but I know
his touch too, so maybe it will be OK.

What's on the next sheets cost a lot of lives and years to
get; it's the genuine article.

Now I'm going to take one more look, and remember
some things, so when the choice gets tough I'll know which
one to make. Then I'm going in, and I won't be back this
way.

8

The drawing on the sheet tacked to the back of the note
showed me the valley and the lake and a spot on the north
side that matched the town, labeled "Keep." There was an X
marking the cougar cave. Another sketch below showed the
details of a door and a shaft cut to below the valley floor, and
a tunnel down there that crossed to the Keep and then some
more detail on a hatch that led out into a false wall behind a
furnace room. Another page had the layout of the Keep, in-
cluding more dummy passages and double walls than Canter-
ville Castle. They led all the way to a big spread on the top
level, with a couple of alternates and a few question marks,
just to give me the feeling it hadn't all been done for me.

I read it through again, looking for some useful clue I might
have missed, but I didn't find any more details of what I
was expected to do. There was just the chart and the map,
and the note, full of confidence that all I lived for was the
chance to go where he'd gone and not come back from.

He was quite a guy, was my letter-writer, and he expected
a lot of me. More than he was likely to get.

I was supposed to know a lot of things I didn't know, and
maybe those were the things that would have made me hot
to tighten my belt and go looking for the kind of trouble that
would be waiting for me at the end of that cute tunnel and
those neat rat holes in the walls.

I thought these thoughts for half an hour or so. Then I went

over to the door that was cut into the wall behind the big tank
and got it open and saw steps and started down.

9

There was enough water in the tunnel to make a spotty
reflection of the glow from the ceiling strip and show up the
rats that moved away ahead of me just out of BB gun range.
I stopped a couple of times to listen, in case somebody was
waiting for me up ahead and making noises. I didn't hear anything. That made me feel lonelier than ever.

The tunnel ended at a stair like the one I'd come down.
The steps went up forty feet and ended in a landing just
big enough to stand on. There was a wooden panel in front
of me, with something chalked on the back of it in block letters: HINGES AT LEFT. WATCH FOR TRAFFIC FROM
KITCHEN.

He was still with me. The thought didn't help much. From
here, with all he knew, he'd gone on to get killed, an item
that had probably netted two inches on an inside page; I felt
over the panel, put a little weight against the right edge, then
a little more. Nothing moved. That meant I could go back
home and forget the whole thing. I gave it one last push and
it swung out and dust sifted down and I could see light coming through a vertical space at the end of a passage about a
foot wide between the wall and a slab of sheet metal that
would be the back of the heat plant. Past that, there was a big
room with long tables and cabinets built in along one wall and
a half-open door into another big room with a light and men in
black sitting around a table. Just then something behind me
made a *clack!* like a round sliding into a chamber, and I went
as stiff as Automat Jell-O. Then a blower started up and sheet
metal around me started to thrum. I let some air out and got
my mouth back over my teeth and moved out along the wall.
From here I had a better view of the room beyond the door.
There were four men in there, with cards in their hands. A

clock on the wall over their heads said seven-twenty-eight. It was well into the morning, but there was no sunlight shining in, which meant no windows. I filed that observation away and one of the men laid down his hand and stood up. So did the other three. One of them said something and they moved out of sight, acting like fellows remembering a missed appointment.

I worked my way along the side of the walk-in reefer and located three bolt heads that looked like the other ones but which turned, with a little persuasion, and let a piece of solid-looking wall ride straight back on oiled rails. I pushed in past it into a tight space and got it closed behind me. What I was in now was a tight vertical shaft thirty inches in diameter with six-inch rods going up in a spiral and a smell of old dust. The wall of the shaft and the rods both had the soapy feel of a high polymer plastic. I checked to be sure my gat was riding around front where I could get at it, and started up.

CHAPTER TEN

It was a nice easy climb for the first few dozen turns. Then my back started to ache from the bent-over position and my arches started to feel the rods and my hands were slippery with sweat and it was a long way down. All the light I had to see by was a creepy pale green glow that came from the plastic itself. I reminded myself of one of those restless corpses that grandpa used to tell me about before the DT's got him; the kind they had back in the old country that used to come out from under tombstones on the night of the new moon. Only this time I was the spook. I decided to give up that line of thought before I scared myself to death and just then somebody tapped me on the shoulder.

2

Now, maybe you think a tough Hunky with a gun in his pants can absorb that kind of surprise with no more reaction than a curled lip and a reflex move toward the hip. I made the reflex move OK: I jumped so hard I bent one of the rods an inch out of line with my head and one foot slipped off and I was hanging by my hands looking up at bones.

There was enough light to see a set of fingers and a wrist joint and above that what was left of an arm leading up to some less clearly defined anatomy. There was no flesh there, just the clean yellow-white skeleton, glowing a little, like old neon, in the dark. I made out the skull with the lower jaw hanging wide open as if it was getting ready to take a bite, and the other arm, and the torso and legs, just sort of folded down against the spine, which was broken in two places and doubled back on itself and jammed against the rungs.

I held on there for a while and then got my feet back on the rungs and made three tries and swallowed and felt sweat drip off the end of my nose. I got one hand unglued and reached up and got a grip on Mr. Bones above the wrist and pulled. The forearm came off at the elbow and flopped back and broke at the wrist and small bones made a light clatter going down the shaft. I dropped the ulna and went up a step higher and my face was in front of the spot where the hand had been and there was something on the wall there: a stain in the form of a couple of lines that made a straggly "T". I touched the lines and a dry brownish powder crumbled away. Dried blood. Before he'd died, the skeleton with the broken back had tried to write something, and almost made it.

T. T for Treachery, or for Too late. I couldn't think of anything good that started with a T. T for Trouble, T for Turn back.

T for Trap.

I looked up and the empty sockets met my look. Number

Four; the letter-writer. The letters that had still been there, left there for me to find—like these bones—warning me to look out for trouble ahead; tipping me off that I was walking into ambush. But why hadn't the man that killed him taken the dead mouse out of the trap and dusted off the cheese and set it, all ready for the next one?

Or maybe I was building it all on a set of cold feet. Maybe the skeleton was just a careless carpenter left over from the construction phase. Maybe he was the guy who designed this back stair, tossed in on top of it after it was finished, to seal his lips. And maybe I was a fan dancer.

It had to be the fourth man, because this was his route, and nobody had used it after him, because he was blocking it solidly with his bones. Yeah, maybe that was it. He'd gone up, walked into the trap, taken a load of slugs in the stomach, and then instead of lying down there to die, he'd made it back to his rat hole and fallen down it, so the next man would find him and think what I was thinking.

I looked up past the bones and saw the faint cylindrical shine of the tube, leading on up to the place I had to go, to find the man I had to find.

"Thanks, pal," I said to the skull. I pushed at the bones and they fell away into darkness. The rungs led upward another hundred feet and ended at a door that opened into a small, dark room.

3

I crossed the room without falling over anything much, put an ear to the door. That told me nothing. I eased it open half an inch and looked out into a lighted hall.

There was a Blackie standing with his back to me about twelve feet away. He had a gadget like a stopwatch in his hand and he was aiming it at the wall and his lips were moving. I waited in the shadows until he worked his way close enough. Then I stepped out and he came around fast but too late and I hit him up under the angle of the jaw, the one that breaks the neck if you do it right. My aim was OK. He started his dive and I caught him and took him back into my lair.

It took me ten minutes to get him stripped out and tucked away in the closet, another five to get his pants and coat on. They were a lousy fit, and hadn't been out to the dry cleaner lately. I had to pass the boots; the ones I had on were close enough. I checked his gun, but it had too many colored buttons I didn't know about. I ditched it and tucked Minka's little one in the holster and headed for a door down the hall. I was almost there when a foot scraped behind me and a heavy voice said, "OK, all you culls are wanted up to Comsat on the triple."

I kept going, reached the door, had it halfway open when the voice yelled after me, "OK, Wallik, that means you, too."

I slid inside and was in a tiled room with a dirty window and plumbing. Great. Trapped in the john. The window was two feet high and a foot wide, with obscure glass in it. A light-and-shadow pattern on it looked like bars. It didn't give much light. I got behind the door and palmed the gun and waited. A minute went by. It was quiet outside now. Then feet came across and a fist hit the door and a heavy voice said, "OK, it don't take that long," and the feet went away.

I gave it another five minutes and came out, cautiously. The hall was all mine again. Faint sounds came from the far end of it. I went the other way, found stairs, went up them to a landing, listened, went on up and came out in a wide corridor with lights and open doors to rooms with daylight showing from them. Somebody came out of a door and crossed the hall and went into another door. A typewriter was clacking somewhere. Somebody was arguing with somebody, saying, "I don't care if you've replaced all of them, check them again, high and low scale . . ."

I could see the foot of a wide staircase along the hall. It didn't attract me. I went to the right, checked a plain door that might have been a service stair, was looking at a vacuum cleaner and a shelf with cans and bottles. Maybe it was a good find at that. If the chase got hot I could hide in there and pretend to be a broom.

I went on to the end, turned left, smelled breakfast cooking somewhere. It made my jaws ache. There was a carpet here, and the lighting was recessed and muted, the way it is when there's money around. A Blackie came out of a room ahead and started my way. I took the first door to the left and was in a room with a couple of easy chairs and a divan long enough to sleep two in-laws. A window looked out on a garden with flowers and another wing of the building on the other side. The steps outside went by softly. I waited and then opened up and looked out. He was standing at the intersection, looking back at me. For a long second we stared at each other. Then I winked. He staggered back a step as if I'd hit him in the gut with a wet towel and whirled and disappeared. I came out and went on and a few doors farther found an open elevator door and stepped in and palmed a panel full of buttons and started up.

4

The car went up one floor and stopped and two men got in. I got my fingers over the gun and one of them gave me a hard look and said to the other, "By God, things have changed since I pulled the duty." The other one did some noisy breathing through his nose.

We rode along in silence together and the car stopped and a woman with a pale doughy face got on and the two men got off without looking back. The woman gave me a look and patted her back hair. At the next stop a girl got on and stared at me. She stared at me through two more stops. At the next one a man in a gray coverall got on and she opened her mouth to say something and I said, "Excuse it, kid, I was up all night, and I don't mean walking the baby," and patted her hip going past. Her mouth was still open as the door closed.

There were more people here, moving up and down the hall, which was neat and clean and full of that office smell. Nobody seemed to see me. I went along fast to the end of the hall and found the service stair and went up two flights and dead-ended at a landing that needed sweeping. There was a small window here that showed me a nice sweep of early-morning lawn and the fence in the distance, inconspicuous behind the screen of shrubbery. There seemed to be a lot of Blackies out on the grass. I was estimating my altitude at ten stories now. From outside it hadn't looked that high. The lonesome feeling was back, strong. I hadn't met any live people, to talk to, for quite a few days now. I pushed through a narrow door and out into the whisper of air conditioning and the dead white of artificial light. It was a big room with chairs and tables with magazines on them, like a room where you wait for one of those dentists who hate to talk about money. A hall led away from the other side of it. There was nobody in sight, in the room or in the hall. Everything seemed quieter than it ought to. I looked at two plain wood-slab doors with shiny hardware, and another door with a used look around the knob. It looked friendlier than the others. I went over to it and tried it. It swung in on a swell storeroom full of sealed cartons and a fat voice behind me said "Hey!"

I came around fast with the gun all set to go and a big fellow with eyes bugged behind lenses like biscuits pointed toward the door I came in by and said, "I've warned Alders about you people intruding here!"

"Sorry, chief," I said. "I guess maybe I kind of lost my way—"

"I heard you'd staged another of your ridiculous false alarms —the third this week, wasn't it? Every time a bird flutters over the building looking for a worm it starts bells ringing and lights flashing! You don't delude me with your show of activity! It's all an excuse for prying here in Tabulation!" He grabbed his glasses and pushed them back into his head, like coal eyes on a snowman. With his kind of vision, contacts wouldn't help.

"Yeah, I'll just be on my way. Guess we can't fool you, Doc—"

"Mind your tongue, you! You're aware that I detest that flippant epithet! Has Alders instructed you to add insolence to your other offenses?"

"Sorry, Doctor. I was just on the way out—"

"The other way!" He pointed a finger that was just a little longer than it was thick. I went the way it pointed and had a choice of up or down on a narrow stairway with dope-stick butts. I went up past a little landing with a couple of empties parked in the corner, up six more steps, and was stopped by a black door with panic hardware on it. I tried it and it gave and I came out into brilliant sunshine. I was on the roof. The tower apartment I was looking for wasn't here.

5

In the next five seconds a couple of things happened. The first was that I looked across seventy feet of open space and saw a second tower going up thirty feet higher than the one I was in, with a wide terrace tacked to one corner. The other was a noise off to the left that made me fade back behind the monitor and slide down flat against hot tarred roof.

"What was that?" somebody said.

"What?"

"I thought I heard Waxlow come up."

"You got ten minutes yet."

"I heard—" The door I had come through banged open and feet stepped out.

"Yah! Waxlow, you're early!"

They moved off talking. I sneaked a look. There was nothing on the roof but a platform with what looked like an ack-ack gun except that it had a set of cooling fins along the barrel, and some heavy cable snaking off to a big panel with dials, and on to a standpipe by the parapet. There were three Blackies, all wearing helmets and side arms. They jawed for a few minutes and one of them came back over my way and went through the door and it closed behind him. The other two settled down by the gun and squinted at nothing. One of them yawned. The other one spat. A bird flew over and dropped quano in a white streak and went his way. A fly came and checked me out. I stayed where I was and waited for the big break.

An hour later I was still waiting. Another man came up and relieved one of the Blackies and the other man took a couple of turns around the roof, but I was pretty well hidden in the shadows between the stairhead and a ventilation intake. Another hour went by. All I wanted was ten seconds with both boys in sight and looking the other way so I could sneak back inside, but it was no go.

Lunchtime came and went. The sun beat down and the roof soaked up heat and I sweated inside the black suit, and the tight seams galled me under the arms and around the neck.

The sun came over on the other side and made the boys shift position a little, but not enough. I tried to move a little to get back in the shadow and touched hot roof and raised a blister on my knee.

About midafternoon an NCO came up and poked around the gun and squinted up at the sky and came over and stood four feet from me and belched and went back inside. More reliefs came up. The sun went back of the high tower and I started catching dinner smells from below.

The roof had cooled some by then, and I shifted and got into a better position and could see the terrace across the way. A man's head showed over the edge once, bobbing around as if he were doing something fussy like weeding a flower box or laying a table. A little later lights went on up there and some music floated down. It was twilight now. The sky was a silent pink explosion. The pink deepened and scarlet ships flying purple banners sailed away toward the west. Then there were stars and a chill in the air and a mosquito bit the back of my neck. Over by the gun I could see little red and green and blue lights of instruments that could probably pinpoint a nosy aircraft at fifty miles; but none of them pointed at me, lying doggo twenty feet away.

A bell dinged down below and the watch changed again. When the door opened, a blaze of light shone out. Not much chance of a quiet sneak through that.

At a rough estimate, I'd been pinned in this spot for twelve hours now. The chances for improving my position didn't seem to be getting any better. Another few hours and I'd be too stiff to move and too weak to go anywhere if I did move. It was time to make a play—any play.

From my spot back of the stairhead, the gun emplacement was off to the right, near the parapet. To the left of that, the line ran straight back for thirty feet and then went into a series of setbacks and angled across behind me. The other tower was over that way, just a set of lights floating on the night now. I slid backward and got up on all fours and did a little silent groaning and made it to my feet, with the stairhead and the ventilator between me and the gun crew. The roof surface was smooth but gritty; I took off my boots and shoved them inside my blouse and went over to the parapet and had a look.

6

What I saw wasn't encouraging: A sheer drop of fifty feet to a ledge where light shone out on plants growing in a box and below that another drop of a couple hundred feet to the walled court, looking the size of a five-cent regular issue. Off to the left, a connecting wall went across to the other tower, at the level of the planter ledge. To the right there was a swell view of the string of lights in the distance along the perimeter of the reservation. None of that gave me any ideas. I backed off, feeling that vulnerable feeling that high places give me, and heard a sound that made me spin and grab for the gun and then lights went on all across the roof. They were big dazzlers, mounted on six-foot poles. The air around them looked

like blue smoke and they highlit the shape of every pebble on
the roof like a die-cutter stamping silhouettes out of sheet
steel. There was one patch of shadow, as black as a chimney-
sweep's T-shirt, cast by the doorhead; and I was in it.

The men on the gun were shielding their eyes and swearing
and other men were coming out on the roof and fanning out.
There was no talking; the guns they had in their hands told
me all I needed to know.

They formed up on the far side of the roof and started
across. I had maybe thirty seconds to think up a scheme, check
it over for flaws, and put it into execution. They were almost
over to the stairhead. I backed away, which put the parapet
against the back of my thighs. I didn't think about it; I swung
one leg over and found a toehold in the rough stonework and
ducked and heard feet walk past and stop and come back.
That was enough for me. I got a grip on the ledge I was
squatting on and let my legs down and felt around for a place
to put them, and started down.

7

Two minutes later I was on the ledge I'd seen from above.
It went straight on for forty feet to the fancy corner. The cross
wall to the other tower joined there. I put my cheek to the wall
and went along to the end. Then I turned to put my back to
the wall and jumped for the cross wall. I was prepared to fall
on the roof side if it worked out that way; but I landed square,
went forward on all fours, and headed for the deep shadow
at the far end. The light went past behind me. I reached the
wall and pushed my face hard against it and breathed with
my mouth open. The light traveled back along the ledge and
up the wall again and went out. I sat up and felt around in the
dark and found a heavy stone balustrade, got over that and
was on a narrow terrace with a row of pots big enough for Ali
Baba. Vines were rooted in them, growing thick and black up
the wall. Up above I could see a little light on the railing of

the higher terrace. The vines grew there, too. It looked like it might be possible, for a trained athlete in top condition, with spiked climbing shoes and a Derby winner's luck. I stepped up on the stone railing and got a fistful of tough vine and started up.

The first few feet were as easy as getting into trouble. The main stems were as big as my wrist, and clamped to the wall like British plumbing. Then they branched and I started hearing little ripping sounds. I stopped there for a few minutes with the night breeze blowing across my face and thought about what might be waiting for me up above, versus what I knew was down below. Then I unclamped my hands and tried for new holds higher up.

Half an hour later I got a hand on the bright-plated railing of the upper balcony just as the pencil-thick creeper I was hanging onto let go. There were a few seconds of fast living then, while I grabbed for a two-handed grip and waited for my life to flash before my eyes. Then I was hanging on by a knee and an elbow, looking across polished tiles into a deep room full of subdued light and oiled teak paneling, and a desk no bigger than a Cadillac with a man sitting at it, facing away from me. He was leaning back in the chair, smoking a cigaret. He had a wide back and a solid neck and a little gray in his hair. As far as I could tell, he was alone. While I looked at him, he reached and stubbed the butt out in an ashtray hewn out of a chunk of glass the size of a football. Then he pushed a button and a drawer slid open and up and he lifted a big decanter and poured dark brandy into a glass and while both hands were busy stoppering the decanter I came up and over the rail and slid the gun into my hand and went over to the open doors behind him and said, "Don't even breathe, pal."

He checked, just for an instant; then he hit the stopper with his palm and put the jug back in the drawer and swung around to face me.

The man I was looking at was me.

CHAPTER ELEVEN

For about ten seconds we stared at each other; then I saw that he wasn't so much looking at me as he was giving me a chance to look at him. He was something to look at.

I've never had a delicate look, but this face was hewn out of the earth's primordial rock, weathered to a saddle brown and lined a little by time's erosion, then polished with a hand finer than Cellini's to a portrait of power held in restraint. He could have been anywhere from a tough forty-five to a smooth sixty. He was wearing a wine-colored dressing gown with a black collar; his neck projected from it like the trunk of an oak tree. His expression was somewhere between a smile too faint to see and no expression at all.

"All right, you got here," he said in my voice. "Come in and sit down. We have things to talk about."

I moved a step and then remembered I was giving the orders. "Stand up and move away from the desk," I said. "Do it nice and easy. I'm not good enough with this thing to try any near-misses."

He pushed the corners of his mouth up half a millimeter and didn't move. "I tried to find you before you took the risk of coming here—"

"Your boys are second-rate. Soft from too much easy duty, maybe." I motioned with the gun. "I won't tell you three times."

He shook his head; or maybe my eyelid quivered. He wasn't a guy to waste effort on a lot of unnecessary facial expressions.

"You didn't come here to shoot me," he said.

"I could change my plans. Being here makes me nervous. Not having you cooperate makes me even more nervous. When I'm nervous I do some dumb things. I'm going to do one now." I raised the gun and aimed it between his eyes and was squeezing and he came out of the chair fast. He gave me a big smile. You could almost see it.

"If I'd meant to hurt you, I could have done it any time since you crossed the line," he said. "It's wired—"

"The perimeter fence, maybe; not inside. Your own troops would be tripping it a hundred times a day."

"You think you could have gotten this far without my knowing it?"

"You can't lock the world out unless you lock yourself in. Eighty years of waiting could make a man careless."

He gave me a little frown to look at. "Who do you think I am?"

"There are some holes in the picture," I said. "But the part that's there says you're a guy I used to know. His name was Steve Dravek."

"But you're Steve Dravek." He said it the way you tell a kid his dog died.

"I just think I'm Steve Dravek," I told him. "You're the real article."

He frowned a little more. "You mean—you think I'm the original Dravek, born in 1941?"

"It sounds a little funny," I said. "But that's what I think."

He tilted his head a quarter of an inch and did something subtle that changed the frown back into a smile.

"No wonder you're nervous," he said. "My God, boy, put the gun down and sit down and have a drink. I'm not Number One; I'm Number Five!"

2

I moved around him to a chair and waved him to one and watched him sit, and then I sat, and rested the gun on my knee so the shaky hand wouldn't be so obvious. I wanted a drink the way Romeo wanted Juliet.

"What happened to Four?"

"What you'd expect. He was past his prime—over fifty. I

tried to talk to him, but he wouldn't talk. Why should he? He owned the world."

"That would be how long ago?"

"Over forty years. As soon as I'd established myself here— there was a certain amount of pretty delicate maneuvering involved there—I tried to find out if there were any more of us. I drew a blank." He almost blinked. "Until you turned up."

"Tell me about that part."

"The tanks were rigged to signal when they were opened from the inside; just one quick squawk on the microwave band. You'd have to know just where to listen to pick it up. Unfortunately, there was no R and D feature; just the signal saying you were on the way. I tried to find you, but you dropped out of sight."

"It seemed like a good idea; even if your Blackies are lousy shots."

"They were instructed to fire anesthetic pellets."

"Some of those pellets packed quite a wallop."

He nodded. "It was too bad about that little man, Jess Ralph; when the men surprised you there, they jumped to a couple of conclusions—"

"Somebody tipped them. They were waiting."

"Naturally the ETORP reserve is under close guard—"

"Pass that. If you wanted to talk to me, why didn't you leave a message where I'd find it? You would have known where. And it would have been simpler than telling your Blackies to wing me with a needle full of dope."

"Would you have trusted me? As I remember the final instructions Frazier added to my 'cephtape, they painted a pretty black picture of the Old Man. I thought it was better to handle it as I did, let you follow the same trail I did. And it had the added advantage of bringing you here in secret. I think you can see it might complicate things to have the word get out that there were two of us."

"Uh-huh," I said, "maybe. By the way, let's see your wrist."

He looked thoughtful. Then he turned back his right cuff and showed it to me.

"It was the other one, remember?"

He showed me that one. The skin was perfect; there was no sign of the scar that only Number One would have.

"Satisfied now?" He was looking a little more relaxed. Maybe I was, too.

"Suppose you're telling the truth," I said. "How does that change things?"

"It ought to be pretty plain. The Old Man was nuts, power-crazy. I don't share that part of his personality."

"You took over where he left off," I said. "Nothing's changed."

"The world he built wasn't something I could rebuild in a day. It all takes time; if I tried to reform the whole thing at once, I'd have chaos on my hands."

"I got the feeling things were getting worse instead of better."

"It's not surprising you had a few wrong slants, considering the company you were keeping."

"What company would that be?"

"The little man, Jess. I thought you knew. He was Frazier's grandson."

3

"There seem to be a lot of things I don't know," I said. "Maybe by the time it got to be my turn the brainwashing machine was slipping its clutch. Maybe you'd better give me the whole story, right from the top."

His face tightened and his eyes looked at me and beyond me into the past.

"The first part of it, I remember myself, as if it was really me it happened to—the tapes Frazier took were good ones. Every detail is there, as if it had happened yesterday . . .

"It started like any other morning. I had breakfast out on

the terrace with Marion, drove to the plant, spent some time going over some tax figures with Frazier; then we went down to the new basement wing to see how things were going. It was a big pilot rig for a new process that was going to make us a mint. A new principle that would put us years ahead of anything else on the market.

"It was about half past ten when it happened. Marion was on the way into the city to do some shopping. The kid was with her. They stopped because she had some flowers she'd picked for me. White daisies, the first of the year. There were a lot of them down by the pool . . .

"They went to the office first and when I wasn't there some damned fool told them I was down in the new wing. They came on down.

"Frazier and I were over by the big cryo tank, watching Brownie stitch a plate in. Something slipped, and a piece of quarter-inch got away from the lift and it dropped and cut the high-tension lead from the portable welding rig. There was a lot of arcing and smoke—and right in the middle of it they came in.

"I started over there and waved them away and yelled to them to go back, and she saw me wave and started across and before Marion could grab her, she got into the smoke and lost her bearings, and I yelled to her again to go back and she heard me and turned my way and put a foot on the edge of the plate that was carrying sixty thousand amps.

"I was the first one to her. I grabbed her and yelled for the plant doc and the son of a bitch was off playing golf and there wasn't anybody else near enough to do any good. She wasn't breathing; there was no pulse. I knew five minutes of that and her brain would be gone forever . . .

"I did the only thing I could do. We had a liquid nitrogen setup running in glass. I took her in there and told Frazier to get the top off the big receiver tank. He argued and I knocked him down. They all thought I'd gone nuts. I got it open myself and came back and Marion was holding her and wouldn't let her go. I had to take her. I carried her in and injected her and got her wrapped and put her inside and closed up and charged the coils and watched the plate frost over. In less than a minute it was done. Then I came back out and they were waiting for me, with guns and a cop they'd gotten in from somewhere. I could have torn 'em apart with my bare hands, but I knew I couldn't afford any mistakes now. She was in there, frozen, at six degrees Kelvin; but it was no good unless I convinced them I knew what I was doing, that it was the only chance.

"I talked to them. I kept calm and I talked to them and told them the kid was dead, and that what I'd done hadn't killed her any deader; and that as long as they left her where I'd put her, she'd stay just the way she was then. If any damage had been done, it was already done, and if it hadn't—well, if it hadn't, it was up to the medics to find out how to bring her back. And that meanwhile she stayed where she was.

"Frazier was the first to see it and side me. He'd been crazy about the kid. He got them under control and cleared the cops out and got a bunch of big-domes from Mayo over there and I went back home and drank a year's supply of booze in the next week. I didn't know where Marion was. They said I'd hit her pretty hard. But I wasn't thinking about Marion. I was only thinking about the kid.

"Some sob sisters got hold of it, then, and the newspapers got into it, and I was indicted for everything from murder to grave-robbery. There were laws that said a body had to be buried within two days, and a lot of other junk.

"Well, I beat 'em. She was underground. The research wing was twelve feet down. And I had witnesses that there was no pulse and no breathing. The papers kept playing the story for a few months, but after a while that stopped, too.

"I had the room where it had happened walled off. I never wanted to see it again.

"We went ahead with the new process, and it worked out like I said it would. Food quick-frozen to under ten degrees

K would keep forever, and come out as if it had been fresh that morning. Even the leafy stuff, lettuce and potatoes; everything. In a year we had a hundred licensees. In two years we'd stopped licensing and had our own plants, in forty-two countries. I poured every dime back into research, and the more we learned the quicker we learned. I didn't give a damn about the business; all I wanted was the money and the know-how to push the medical program. I went on working like six demons and waiting for the day the docs would give me the go-ahead.

"But they were a cagey bunch. In a year they told me they thought they were on the right track. In two, they were talking about breakthroughs. In five, it was unanticipated complexities in the mechanics of submolecular crystallization. By the time they'd been at it for ten years, to the tune of a hundred million a year, they were doing a lot of cute tricks with frozen mice and cats and lambs and telling me about critical thresholds and optimum permeability mass-ratios and energy transference rates and all the other gobbledegook their kind use to keep the layman shelling out.

"I called for a showdown, and they said, of course, Mr. Dravek, certainly, Mr. Dravek, whatever you say, Mr. Dravek. But we won't be responsible . . .

"What could I do? I hired and fired medical directors like baseball managers, but they all gave me the same pitch; wait another year just to be on the safe side. . . . Five more years went by, and another five, and meanwhile Draco Incorporated had grown into the biggest international combine on earth. We were in foods and medicines and the equipment that went with them, and had sidelines that were bigger than most of the world's industrial giants. The government had tried to step in ten different times to break us, but by then I'd made some interesting discoveries about politicians. They bribe easy, and a lot cheaper than you'd think. And for the big boys—the ones who would have laughed at money—we had some other little items. Those sawbones hadn't been just rolling pills; they'd come up with tricks that could make a man look and feel twenty years younger; and the Draco Foundation had been doing a lot with grafts and regeneration. We didn't publicize all this. It was strictly hush-hush, behind-the-walls stuff. Only our friends got in on it. And by then we didn't have a lot of enemies. So they left us alone, and I waited, and now they were talking about next year, maybe, and then a few more months and we'll be ready to take the chance . . .

"You see, by then they had the techniques for deep-freezing and thawing. Hell, we were doing it on a commercial scale. But we were doing it under controlled cryolab conditions, with everything from tissue salinity to residual muscular electric charge controlled every step of the way.

"But with the kid, I hadn't had time for anything fancy. I'd just injected her with an anti-crystallizer we used in vegetable processing and put her under. That made it different. It gave them an excuse to stall. Because that's what they were doing. Stalling. They figured as soon as I had her back, I'd pull the rug out from under their operation. The damned fools! As if I'd sabotage the program that had made me the richest tycoon that ever lived—and with the power to appoint the whole damned Supreme Court if I'd wanted to!

"So they stalled me. And I was getting older. By then it was 2003; I was over sixty, not that I looked it. Like I said, the pill rollers had come up with some tricks. But I knew I couldn't last forever. And I had a board of directors who were looking ahead, jockeying for the day when one of them would take over where I left off. I knew if I dropped dead the day would never come for the kid. They'd leave her there. Because she was my heir, you see? If she was alive, she'd own it all, and they'd be cut out of the pattern. So I had to do something. I had to work out a plan that would carry on after my death, so some day she'd come back, and find her inheritance waiting for her.

"I thought about it, and worked out one plan and then another, and none of 'em were any good, none of 'em were foolproof. Because there was no way to be sure there'd be a man there I could trust. Frazier would have done it, but he was my age; he wouldn't outlast me long. And anyway, the only man I could really trust was—me. And that gave me the idea.

"I called in my Chief of Research and told him what I wanted. He told me I was out of my mind. I said, sure, Doc, but can you do it?

"He was a long time coming around, but in the end he had to admit there was no reason it was impossible. Illegal, maybe —we'd had some trouble with a bunch of fanatics and we'd had to let a few token laws get on the books—but it wasn't any trickier than what we'd been doing for some of our chums in Congress.

"It was simple enough. We'd been using test tube techniques for growing livestock for a long time; our brood plant in Arizona covered ten acres and produced more beef in a year than the State of Texas used to in ten. They took germ cells from me and started them growing, then planted them in automated life support tanks, like the stock brooders, only fancier. I gave Frazier the job of picking the spots for the vaults to be built out of indetectable nonmetallic material. I gave him orders not even to tell me. That way nobody could squeeze the secret out of me, or step in and act in my name and break up the playhouse; because I didn't know myself where they were.

"The first duplicate was rigged to mature in twenty years. I figured to be around that long. I'd brief him myself, and he'd take over from me, and they could scratch their heads and say that the Old Man was holding up a lot better than anybody figured; and when he'd run his time, the next one would be ready; and so on down the line, until the medics were ready to unfreeze the child. They could stall a long time, but they couldn't stall forever. And when they quit stalling, I'd be ready."

The man behind the desk took a deep breath and looked at me.

"That's where my tape ended. I came to in an abandoned mine shaft in Utah. The tank was set back into a side passage and covered over. There was information waiting for me, food, a full briefing up to the time Frazier had last been there, about 2020. The rest of the story I had to put together from the Old Man's records.

"It was a swell plan he'd worked out; practically perfect. Just one thing went wrong. He got a hurry-up call from the Old Lab one day. He went over and they told him all bets were off. There'd been a freak power failure and the special tank she was in had lost its chill and the body had been at about a degree Centigrade for a couple of hours when they discovered it. So now Duna was just a corpse like any other corpse. She looked the same, but that little spark they'd been keeping alive all those years—or trying to—was gone.

"It hit him hard, but not as hard as it had the first time. Over thirty years had gone by. He'd learned to live with it. She'd been the biggest thing in his life, once; he could still lie awake at night and remember her voice, the look on her face when she'd come running to meet him when he came home. But that was all it was: just a recollecton out of a fairy tale that he'd had once, a long time ago, and lost forever.

"He gave orders to Frazier for the body to be embalmed and buried; but by then Frazier was a little nuts on the subject. He didn't believe the medics. He wanted them to go ahead with the thaw, and when the Old Man wouldn't, he said some things to him that he'd have killed any other man for. Then he left.

"The Old Man went on with the funeral. And just before the grave was closed he had a thought and told them to open the box, and they did; and it was empty. Or almost empty. There was a little scale model of some kind of Indian temple in it, made out of solid gold. Frazier's idea of a joke, maybe. he'd been a good man once, but he was getting old. The Old Man tried to find him, but couldn't. He'd made some plans of his own. He was quite a boy, was Frazier. A billionaire in his own right. He knew how to cover a trail.

"So the Old Man called off the hunt. Frazier had been a good friend for a lot of years. It was too bad he'd gone off his rocker in his old age, but the thing to do was let it go and forget it. As for the body—well, it was just a body now; in time Frazier would realize that and bury it and it would all be over.

"Meanwhile, there was a business to run. In a way, it was a relief to the Old Man to have the other off his mind. He'd been living in the past too long, trying to hold onto a dream that was a long time dying. Now he could put all his efforts into the important things.

"By this time the food processing empire was the tail that was trying to wag the dog. The sidelines were the big business. Rejuvenation methods that could keep a man looking young at ninety; artificial organs that he manufactured under his own patents—and some he didn't even patent, because he didn't want any information leaks through the Patent Office. That was where the money was—and the power.

"After that things moved fast. The Old Man was already running the United States; he branched out then, took control of the French Assembly, then the Scandinavian Parliament, most of South America, Africa, Southeast Asia. He changed the name of the company, and reorganized it along lines that took control out of the hands of the board and put it where it belonged—in his pocket."

"You said you changed the company's name," I butted in. I already knew the answer, but I wanted to hear it from him.

"The Draco Company was all right for a small food-processing firm," he said. "When the outfit grew and moved into the life sciences field, the Old Man decided he needed something with a little more *élan*. He came up with Eternity, Incorporated."

"Commonly known as ETORP," I said.

He nodded. "He had it all in the palm of his hand; and then one day a man came gunning for him.

"The Plan; the one he'd worked out to insure that things were done his way, even after he died—was backfiring on him. Frazier's work. He'd been the one who set it up; he was the one the Old Man trusted. He'd matured the duplicate Dravek in an LS tank and briefed him to kill. It was a clever scheme. Who else was tough enough to kill Dravek—but Dravek?

"But it didn't work. Dravek Number Two found the Old Man; but the Old Man was too smart for him. He shot first. He had the body dumped where it would be found, so Frazier would hear about it and get the message.

"But Frazier was stubborn. Eighteen years later, another killer made his try. He went the same way. This time the Old Man knew Frazier had to go. He spent three years and a billion dollars, and he found him. But the medics weren't quick enough, and all he got out of him was the one fact: That each vault was set to signal when it opened. He got the details on that and nothing else.

"But when Number Three came out, he was ready for him. He was well over a hundred years old now, and still vigorous, but time was running out. He wanted an heir. So when Three showed, he knocked him out with a sleep gun; and when he came out of it, he told him the story. And he took him in and treated him like a son.

"A few months later the Old Man died in his sleep and Number Three went on where he'd left off.

"But the machine was still grinding. Twenty years later, Number Four came along. There was an accident. Three was killed. And then I showed up.

"I guess Number Four was a little greedy. He didn't try to talk to me, just took a shot at me. But my aim was better.

"Things ran quietly for quite a long time. There were problems, but what Dravek Number One could do, Number Five could do again. I had an idea there'd be a Number Six along, about twenty years back, but he never showed up. I figured the Draveks were all used up. And then you came."

"And where do you figure we go from here?"

"I'm not quite as greedy as Four was, Steve. And like the Old Man, I'm getting along to an age where I'm thinking of an heir. I don't have a son."

"Make it plainer."

"There's plenty here for both of us. In a way, you have as much right to it as I do. I want you to stay; share it with me. The whole world, Steve—and everything that's in it . . ."

He leaned toward me, and some of the deadness had gone out of his eyes, and the smile he was playing with was starting to be a real smile.

"I've got a lot to show you, Steve, a lot to tell you . . ." His hand went out to the little table beside him and dipped into the recess under it, and I brought the gun up from my side and shot him through the chest.

CHAPTER TWELVE

The shock half-spun him, knocked him out of the chair. I went after him fast, ready to fire again, but his face already had death written across it. His hand opened and the little silver-framed picture in it fell to the rug. The sleeve that had slid back when he reached was still pulled back almost to the elbow, and I could see the faint white line that ran all the way around his forearm six inches above the wrist.

"Whose arm did you steal, Old Man?" I got the words out. "Number Two's? Or weren't your boys good enough at their graft techniques back then?"

His head turned half an inch. His eyes found me.

"Why . . . ?"

I stooped and picked up the picture he had reached for. "I thought you were trying for your gun," I said. "But it would have ended that way anyway, as long as we had this between us."

A light crossed his face, like a cloud shadow crossing a field of grain.

"Dead," he gasped out. "Dead . . . long . . . ago . . ."

"She's alive, Old Man."

His eyes were holding mine, holding back death.

"Why did you do it, Old Man?" I gave him back his look. "Afraid a living heir might get in your way, after you'd learned how to make yourself immortal?"

He tried to speak, failed, tried again:

"Searched . . . all these years . . . never knew . . ."

"Frazier outsmarted you after all. You ran the world, but in the end he took it away from you. I wonder what your boys did to him, to try to get him to talk. But he never did. He was loyal to you, Old Man, even after you'd stopped being loyal to yourself."

His face was the color of old ivory under the tan. His mouth opened and moved. I stooped to hear him.

"Tell Duna I said . . . hello . . ." His eyes were still on mine, dead eyes now, claiming their last wish.

"Sure," I said. "I'll tell her."

EPILOGUE

They brought Duna up from the vault under the ridge where Frazier had hidden her, and for forty-eight hours the best brains in ETORP's cryothesia lab worked over her. Then they called me in and I was there when she opened her eyes and smiled and said, "Daddy, I brought you some flowers."

That was twenty years ago. She's grown now, and a member of the first Mars Expedition. All the programs that had been stalled for a hundred and fifty years are moving ahead now, pushed by a force of nature that's like the grass root that cracks open a mountainside: population pressure.

I released the immortality drug for general distribution, free, the same day I opened the Ice Palace and started bringing the Old Ones out. Some talk has started up that I ought to reconvene Congress and hand the reins back over to the politicians, but I've got a theory that the world's not ready for that yet. I've set up a system that makes education tapes available to everybody, as many as they can absorb, on any subject. Some day I'll see signs that the race is growing up, and that there are men around who are wise instead of just smart; when that day comes, I'll retire and take that trip to Alpha, if I'm still around. Maybe that's arrogance; or maybe it's a sense of responsibility. Sometimes it's hard to tell the difference.

The Old Man kept a journal. It gave me the answers to a lot of questions that had been on my mind. The skeleton in the shaft was Number Five. He'd been shot, but managed a getaway back into the shaft via a fake air intake in the top-floor equipment room. It didn't look big enough, but it was. He killed two Blackies on the way out, and no one saw where he went; so he kept his secret. The Old Man thought he'd gotten away clean.

The reason the Old Man hadn't closed off the route in via the tunnel was the easy one: he never found it. Frazier had concealed it so it would stay concealed.

The dead boy Jess and I had found was Number Two. He'd killed him and left him like that, as a warning to the next one; if there was a next one. By that time, he was a worried man. And then he had another idea: he meant what he said about taking me in. He wanted somebody else to do the sitting up nights, while he had a brain transfer to a new body—a young, anonymous one—and settled back to enjoy owning the world.

I brought Minka to the Keep, and married her. She and Duna got along swell. They should have. She was Marion's great-granddaughter, which made Duna some kind of great aunt. She told me about Jess and his Secret Society. It didn't amount to much, after being handed down by word-of-mouth tradition for four generations. Most of it had been forgotten, and anyway, Frazier hadn't tried to saddle his descendants with a load of fossilized hates. But he'd left them the job of fighting ETORP, any way they could. Jess's way was hunting Blackies in the park. As I said, Jess was a guy who was full of surprises.

There was one thing that stumped me for a long time: how had Frazier gotten the jump on his boss, gotten the frozen child away from him? But I finally worked it out. Back in the early years, when the Old Man had had about the same life expectancy as the rest of the race, he'd set up a corporation to take over his affairs after his death, and operate it in Duna's name, hold it in trust for her until she was revived. He'd used all the pressure he had to set it up so it couldn't be broken, and to hire the best brains he could buy to run it.

It was a good idea—until the day when his top medical boys told him they'd cracked the Big One, and that now a chosen few could go on living as long as ETORP and its labs held out. That made a difference. He didn't need an heir, then.

By that time, there was a power struggle going on inside the organization that would have made the battle among Alexander's successors look like a pillow fight. That charter—and Duna, alive—was all the opposition needed to take over ETORP, lock, stock, and freeze tanks. And he couldn't have that. In the end Frazier realized the Old Man wouldn't be content for very long to have that small body waiting in the vault, hanging over him day and night; in the end he'd have turned the switch himself.

So Frazier set up the fake equipment failure, the phony funeral, and took Duna to a place where she'd be safe. The Old Man had really believed Duna was dead.

Oh yeah, one other thing. Yesterday a bell rang in a private alert station that's manned twenty-four hours a day, just down the hall from where I sleep. Number Eight is awake and moving—somewhere. I've sent my men out to try to find him, but he seems to be an elusive character.

I'm waiting for him now. When he shows up, I hope I can convince him that what I'm doing is the right thing. If I can't—well, I've got all the weight on my side, but Steve Dravek at twenty was a hard man to beat.

We'll see.

THUNDERHEAD

It was a small room, with an uneven floor, exposed, hand-hewn ceiling beams, a rough fieldstone fireplace. There was furniture: a narrow bunk, a table, a bookcase, straight-backed chairs, all meticulously dusted. A pot of sickly snow-flowers stood in the center of the table. A thick quartz window in a vacuum-tight alloy frame was set in the south wall—a salvaged DV port from a deep-space liner. The view through the window was of black night, whirling snowflakes, a moonlit mountain peak thrusting up toward the sprawling configuration of the constellation *Angina Doloris*.

Beside the window, a compact Navy issue WFP transmitter was set up on a small gray-metal desk. The man standing before it was tall, wide-shouldered, with graying hair, still straight-backed, but thickening through the body now. He studied the half-dozen instrument faces, then seated himself, began noting their readings in a worn notebook. As he worked, the teen-aged boy who stood beside him watched intently.

"I've been working on my Blue codes, Lieutenant Carnaby," the lad was saying. "I'll bet I could pass the Academy exam now." His eager tone changed. "You s'pose I'll ever get the chance, Lieutenant?"

"Sure, Terry," Carnaby said. His voice was deep, husky. "A Navy ship's bound to call here, any time now."

The boy stood by as Carnaby depressed the tape key which would send the recorded call letters of the one-man station flashing outward as a shaped wavefront, propagated at the square of the speed of light.

"Lieutenant," the boy said, "every night you send out your call. How come you never get an answer?"

Carnaby shook his head. "I don't know, Terry. Maybe

they're too busy fighting the Djann to check in with every little JN beacon station on the Outline."

"You said after five years they were supposed to come back and pick you up," the boy persisted. "Why—"

There was a sharp, wavering tone from the round, wire-mesh covered speaker. A dull red light winked on, blinked in a rapid flutter, settled down to a steady glow. The audio signal firmed to a raucous buzz.

"Lieutenant!" Terry blurted. "Something's coming in!"

Swiftly, Carnaby thumbed the big S-R key to RECEIVE, flipped the selector lever to UNSC, snapped a switch tagged RCD.

"*. . . riority, to all stations,*" a voice faint with distance whispered through a rasp and crackle of star-static. "*Cincsec One-two-oh to . . . Cincfleet Nine . . . serial one-oh-four . . . stations copy . . . Terem Aldo . . . Terem . . . pha . . . this message . . . two . . . Part One . . .*"

"What is it, Lieutenant?" The boy's voice broke with excitement.

"A Fleet Action signal," Carnaby said tensely. "An all-station, recorded. I'm taping it; if they repeat it a couple of times, I'll get it all."

They listened, heads close to the speaker grille; the voice faded and swelled. It reached the end of the message, began again: "*Red priority . . . tions . . . incsec One-two . . .*"

The message repeated five times; then the voice ceased. The wavering carrier hum went on another five seconds, cut off. The red light winked out. Carnaby flipped over the SEND key, twisted the selector to VOC-SQ.

"*JN 37 Ace Trey to Cincsec One-two-oh,*" he transmitted in a tense voice. "*Acknowledging receipt Fleet TX 104. Request clarification.*"

Then he waited, his face taut, for a reply to his transmission, which had been automatically taped, condensed to a one-microsecond squawk, and repeated ten times at one-second intervals.

"No good," Carnaby shook his head after a silent minute had passed. "From the sound of the Fleet beam, Cincsec One-two-oh must be a long way from here."

"Try again, Lieutenant! Tell 'em you're here, tell 'em it's time they came back for you! Tell 'em—"

"They can't hear me, Terry." Carnaby's face was tight. "I haven't got the power to punch across that kind of distance." He keyed the playback. The filtered composite signal came through clearly now:

"Red priority to all stations. Cincsec One-two-oh to Rim HQ via Cincfleet Nine-two. All Fleet stations copy. Pass to Terem Aldo Cerise, Terem Alpha Two, and ancillaries. This message in two parts. Part one: CTF Forty-one reports breakthrough of Djann armed tender on standard vector three-three-seven, mark; three-oh-five, mark; oh-four-two. This is a Category One Alert. Code G applies. Class Four through Nine stations stand by on Status Green. Part Two. Inner Warning Line units divert all traffic lanes three-four through seven-one. Outer Beacon Line stations activate main beacon, pulsing code schedule gamma eight. Message ends. All stations acknowledge."

"What's all that mean, Lieutenant?" Terry's eyes seemed to bulge with excitement.

"It means I'm going to get some exercise, Terry."

"Exercise how?"

Carnaby took out a handkerchief and wiped it across his forehead. "That was a general order from Sector Command. Looks like they've got a rogue bogie on the loose. I've got to put the beacon on the air."

He turned to look out through the window toward the towering ramparts of the nine-thousand-foot volcanic peak gleaming white in the light of the small, brilliant moon. Terry followed Carnaby's glance.

"Gosh, Lieutenant—you mean you got to climb old Thunderhead?"

"That's where I set the beacon up, Terry," Carnaby said mildly. "On the highest ground around."

"Sure—but your flitter was working then!"

"It's not such a tough climb, Terry. I've made it a few times, just to check on things." He was studying the rugged contour of the moonlit steep, which resembled nothing so much as a mass of snowy cumulus. There was snow on the high ledges, but the wind would have scoured the east face clear.

"Not in the last five years, you haven't, Lieutenant!" Terry sounded agitated.

"I haven't had a Category One Alert, either," Carnaby smiled.

"Maybe they didn't mean you," Terry said.

"They called for Outer Beacon Line stations. That's me."

"They don't expect you to do it on foot," Terry protested. "Not this time o' year!"

Carnaby looked at the boy, smiling slightly. "I guess maybe they do, Terry."

"Then they're wrong!" Terry's thin face looked pale. "Don't go, Lieutenant!"

"It's my job, Terry. It's what I'm here for. You know that."

"What if you never got the message?" Terry countered. "What if the radio went on the blink, like all the rest of the stuff you brought in here with you—the flitter, and the food unit, and the scooter? Then nobody'd expect you to get yourself killed—"

"But it didn't," Carnaby reminded him gently.

Terry stared at the older man; his mouth worked as though he wanted to speak, but couldn't find the words. "I'll go with you," he said.

Carnaby shook his head. "Thanks, Terry. But you're just a boy. I need a man along on this trip."

Terry's narrow face tightened. "Boy, hell," he said defiantly. "I'm seventeen!"

"I didn't mean anything, Terry. Just that I need a man who's had some trail experience."

"How'm I going to get any trail experience, Lieutenant, if I don't start sometime?"

"Better to start with an easier climb than Thunderhead," Carnaby said gently. "You better go along home now, Terry. Your uncle will be getting worried."

"When . . . when you leaving, Lieutenant?"

"Early. I'll need all the daylight I can get to make Halliday's Roost by sundown."

2

After the boy had gone, Carnaby went to the storage room at the rear of the small house, checked over the meager store of issue supplies. He examined the cold-suit, shook his head over the brittleness of the wiring. At least it had been a loose fit; he'd still be able to get into it.

He left the house then, walked alone up the steep, unpaved street, past the half-dozen ramshackle stores that made up the business district of the single surviving settlement on the frontier planet Longone.

At Maverik's store, the evening's card game had broken up, but half a dozen men still sat around the old hydrogen space heater. They looked up casually.

"I need a man," Carnaby said without preamble. "I've got a climb to make in the morning. A Fleet unit in Deep Space has scared up a Djann blockade runner. My orders are to activate the beacon."

"Orders, eh?" Sal Maverik spoke up. He was a big-faced man with quick, sly eyes. "I don't reckon any promotion orders were included?" He was grinning openly at Carnaby.

"Not this time," Carnaby said mildly.

"Twenty-one years in grade," Sal said genially. "Must be some kind of record." He took out a toothpick and plied it on a back tooth. "Twenty-one years, with no transfer, no replacement, not even a letter from home. I figured they'd forgot you're out here, Carnaby."

"Shut up, Sal." The man named Harry frowned at Carnaby.

"Orders, you said, Jim? You mean you picked up a Navy signal?"

Carnaby nodded. "I just need a man along to help me pack gear as far as Halliday's Roost."

"You gone nuts, Carnaby?" Sal Maverik growled. "Nobody in his right mind would tackle that damned rock after first snow, even if he had a reason."

"Halliday's hut ought to still be standing," Carnaby said. "We can overnight there, and—"

"Jimmy, wait a minute," Harry said. "All this about orders, and climbing old Thunderhead; it don't make sense! You mean after all these years they pick you to pull a damn fool stunt like that?"

"It's a general order to all Outer Line stations. They don't know my flitter's out of action."

Harry shook his head. "Forget it, Jimmy. Nobody can make a climb like that at this time of year."

"Fleet wants that beacon on the air," Carnaby said. "I guess they've got a reason; maybe a good reason."

Maverik spat loudly in the direction of a sand-filled can. "You been sporting that badge for the last twenty years around here," he said. "It's time you turned it in, Carnaby." He riffled the cards in his hands. "I'll play you a hand of showdown for it."

Carnaby rubbed a thumb across the tiny jeweled comet in his lapel, smiled slightly. "Fleet property, Sal," he said.

The big-faced man showed a glint of gold tooth in a sardonic smile. "Yeah," he said. "I guess I forgot."

"Listen, Jim," Harry said urgently. "I remember when you first came here, a young kid still in your twenties, fresh out of the Academy. Five years you was to be here; they've left you to rot for twenty! Now they come in with this piece of tomfoolery. Well, to hell with 'em! After five years, all bets were off. You got no call to risk your neck—"

"It's still my job, Harry."

Harry rose and came over to Carnaby. He put a hand on

the big man's shoulder. "Let's quit pretending, Jim," he said softly. "They're never coming back for you, you know that. The high tide of the Concordiat dropped you here. For twenty years the traffic's been getting sparser, the transmitters dropping off the air. Adobe's deserted now, and Petreac. Another few years and Longone'll be dead, too."

"We're not dead yet."

"That message might have come from the other end of the Galaxy, Jim! For all you know, it's been on the way for a hundred years!"

Carnaby faced him, a big, solidly-built man with a lined face. "You could be right on all counts," he said. "It wouldn't change anything."

Harry sighed, turned away. "If I was twenty years younger, I might go along, just to keep you company, Jimmy. But I'm not. I'm old." He turned back to face Carnaby. "Like you, Jim. Too old."

"Thanks anyway, Harry," Carnaby looked at the other men in the room, nodded slowly. "Sal's right," he said. "It's my lookout, and nobody else's." He turned and pushed back out into the windy street, headed home to make his preparations for the climb.

3

Aboard the Armed Picket *Malthusa*, five million tons, nine months out of Fleet HQ at Van Diemen's World on a routine Deep Space sweep, Signal Lieutenant Pryor, junior communications officer on message deck duty, listened to the playback of the brief transmission the duty NCOIC had called to his attention:

"*JN 37 Ace Trey to Cincsec One . . . Fleet TX . . . clarification,*" the voice came through with much crackling.

"That's all I could get out of it, Lieutenant," the signalman said. "I wouldn't have picked that up, if I hadn't been filtering the Y band looking for AK's on 104."

The officer punched keys, scanned a listing that flashed onto the small screen on his panel.

"There's no JN 37 Ace Trey listed, Charlie," he said. He keyed the playback, listened to the garbled message again.

"Maybe it's some outworld sheepherder amusing himself."

"With WFP equipment? On Y channel?" the NCO furrowed his forehead.

"Yeah." The lieutenant frowned. "See if you can get back to him with a station query, Charlie. See who this guy is."

"I'll try, sir; but he came in with six-millisec lag. That puts him halfway from here to Rim."

The lieutenant crossed the room with the NCO, stood by as the latter sent the standard Confirm ID code. There was no reply.

"I guess we lost him, sir. You want me to log him?"

"No, don't bother."

The big repeater panel chattered then and the officer hurried back to his console, settled down to the tedious business of transmitting follow-up orders to the fifty-seven-hundred Fleet Stations of the Inner Line.

4

The orange sun of Longone was still below the eastern horizon when Carnaby came out the gate to the road. Terry Sickle was there, muffled to his ears in an oversized parka, waiting for him.

"You got to get up early to beat me out, Lieutenant," he said in a tone of forced jocularity.

"What are you doing here, Terry?"

"I heard you still need a man," the lad said, less cocky now.

Carnaby started to shake his head and Terry cut in with: "I can help pack some of the gear you'll need to try the high slope."

"Terry, go on back home, son. That mountain's no place for you."

"How'm I going to qualify for the Fleet when your ship comes, Lieutenant, if I don't start getting some experience?"

"I appreciate it, Terry. It's good to know I have a friend. But—"

"Lieutenant—what's a friend, if he can't help you when you need it?"

"I need you here when I get back, to have a hot meal waiting for me, Terry."

"Lieutenant . . ." All the spring had gone from the boy's stance. "I've known you all my life. All I ever wanted was to be with you, on Navy business. If you go up there, alone . . ."

Carnaby looked at the boy, the dejected slump of his thin shoulders.

"Your uncle know you're here, Terry?"

"Sure. Uh, he thought it was a fine idea, me going with you."

Carnaby looked at the boy's anxious face.

"All right, then, Terry, if you want to," he said at last. "As far as Halliday's Roost."

"Oh, boy, Lieutenant! We'll have a swell time. I'm a good climber, you'll see!" He grinned from ear to ear, squinting through the early gloom at Carnaby. "Hey, Lieutenant, you're rigged out like a real . . ." he broke off. "I thought you'd, uh, wore out all your issue gear," he finished lamely.

"Seemed like for this trek I ought to be in uniform," Carnaby said. "And the coldsuit will feel good, up on the high slopes."

The two moved off down the dark street. The lights were still on in Sal Maverik's general store. The door opened as they came up; Sal emerged, carrying a flour sack, his mackinaw collar turned up around his ears. He swung to stare at Carnaby.

"Hey, by God! Look at him, dressed fit to kill!"

Carnaby and Terry brushed past the thick-set man.

"Carnaby," Sal raised his voice, "was this poor kid the best you could get to hold your hand?"

"What do you mean, poor kid?" Terry started. Carnaby caught his arm.

"We're on official business, Terry," he said. "Eyes front."

"Playing Navy, hah? That's a hot one," the storekeeper called after the two. "What kind of orders you get? To take a goony-bird census, up in the foothills?"

"Don't pay him no attention, Lieutenant," Terry said, his voice unsteady. "He's as full of meanness as a rotten meal-spud is weevils."

"He's had some big disappointments in his life, Terry. That makes a man bitter."

"I guess you did, too, Lieutenant. It ain't made *you* mean." Terry looked sideways at Carnaby. "I don't reckon you beat out the competition to get an Academy appointment and then went through eight years of training just for this." He made a gesture that took in the sweep of the semi-arid landscape stretching away to the big world's far horizon, broken only by the massive outcroppings of the pale, convoluted lava cores spaced at intervals of a few miles along a straight fault line that extended as far as men had explored the desolate world.

Carnaby laughed softly. "No, I had big ideas about seeing the Galaxy, making Fleet Admiral, and coming home covered with gold braid and glory."

"You leave any folks behind, Lieutenant?" Terry inquired, waxing familiar in the comradeship of the trail.

"No wife. There was a girl. And my half brother, Tom. A nice kid. He'd be over forty, now."

The dusky sun was up now, staining the rounded, lumpy flank of Thunderhead a deep scarlet. Carnaby and Sickle crossed the first rock slope, entered the broken ground where the prolific rock lizards eyed them as they approached, then heaved themselves from their perches, scuttled away into the black shadows of the deep crevices opened in the porous rock by the action of ten million years of wind and sand erosion on thermal cracks.

Five hundred feet above the plain, Carnaby looked back at

the settlement; only a mile away, it was almost lost against the titanic spread of empty wilderness.

"Terry, why don't you go on back now," he said. "Your uncle will have a nice breakfast waiting for you."

"I'm looking forward to sleeping out," the boy said confidently. "We better keep pushing, or we won't make the Roost by dark."

5

In the Officers' off-duty bay, Signal Lieutenant Pryor straightened from over the billiard table as the nasal voice of the command deck yeoman broke into the recorded dance music:

"Now hear this. Commodore Broadly will address ship's company."

"Ten to one he says we've lost the bandit," Supply Captain Aaron eyed the annunciator panel.

"Gentlemen," the sonorous tones of the ship's commander sounded relaxed, unhurried. "We now have a clear track on the Djann blockade runner, which indicates he will attempt to evade our Inner Line defenses and lose himself in Rim territory. In this, I propose to disappoint him. I have directed Colonel Lancer to launch interceptors to take up station along a conic, subsuming thirty degrees on axis from the presently constructed vector. We may expect contact in approximately three hours' time." A recorded bos'n's whistle shrilled the end-of-message signal.

"So?" Aaron raised his eyebrows. "A three-million-tonner swats a ten-thousand-ton side-boat. Big deal."

"That boat can punch just as big a hole in the blockade as a Super-D," Pryor said. "Not that the Djann have any of those left to play with."

"We kicked the damned spiders back into their home system ten years ago," Aaron said tiredly. "In my opinion, the whole Containment operation's a boondoggle to justify a ten-million-man Fleet."

"As long as there are any of them alive, they're a threat," Pryor repeated the slogan.

"Well, Broadly sounds as though he's got the bogie in the bag," Aaron yawned.

"Maybe he has," Pryor addressed the ball carefully, sent the ivory sphere cannoning against the target. "He wouldn't go on record with it if he didn't think he was on to a sure thing."

"He's a disappointed 'ceptor jockey. What makes him think that pirate won't duck back of a blind spot and go dead?"

"It's worth a try—and if he nails it, it will be a feather in his cap."

"Another star on his collar, you mean."

"Uh-huh, that too."

"We're wasting our time," Aaron said. "But that's his look-out. Six ball in the corner pocket."

6

As Commodore Broadly turned away from the screen on which he had delivered his position report to the crew of the great war vessel, his eye met that of his executive officer. The latter shifted his gaze uneasily.

"Well, Roy, you expect me to announce to all hands that Cincfleet has committed a major blunder in letting this bandit slip through the picket line?" he demanded with some asperity.

"Certainly not, sir," the officer looked worried. "But in view of the seriousness of the breakout . . ."

"There are some things better kept in the highest command channels," the commodore said shortly. "You and I are aware of the grave consequences of a new release of their damned seed in an uncontaminated sector of the Eastern Arm. But I see no need to arouse the parents, aunts, uncles, and cousins of every apprentice technician aboard by an overly candid disclosure of the facts!"

"I thought Containment had done its job by now," the captain said. "It's been three years since the last Djann sighting outside the Reservation. It seems we're not the only ones who're keeping things under our hats."

Broadly frowned. "Mmmm. I agree, I'm placed at something of a disadvantage in my tactical planning by the oversecretiveness of the General Staff. However, there can be no two opinions as to the correctness of my present course."

The exec glanced ceilingward. "I hope so, sir."

"Having the admiral aboard makes you nervous, does it, Roy?" Broadly said in a tone of heartiness. "Well, I regard it merely as an opportunity better to display *Malthusa's* capabilities!"

"Commodore, you don't think it would be wise to coordinate with the admiral on this—"

"I'm in command of this vessel," Broadly said sharply. "I'm carrying the vice admiral as supercargo, nothing more!"

"He's still Task Group CINC . . ."

"I'm comming this ship, Roy, not Old Carbuncle!" Broadly rocked on his heels, watching the screen where a quadrangle of bright points representing his interceptor squadron fanned out, on an intersecting course with the fleeing Djann vessel. "I'll pinch off this breakthrough single-handed; and all of us will share in the favorable attention the operation will bring us!"

7

In his quarters on the VIP deck, the vice admiral studied the Operational Utter Top Secret despatch which had been handed to him five minutes earlier by his staff signal major.

"It looks as though this is no ordinary boatload of privateers," he looked soberly at the elderly communicator. "They're reported to be carrying a new weapon of unassessed power, and a cargo of spore racks that will knock Containment into the next continuum."

"It doesn't look good, sir," the major wagged his head.

"I note that the commodore has taken action according to the manual." The admiral's voice was noncommittal.

The major frowned. "Let's hope that's sufficient, Admiral."

"It should be. The bogie's only a converted tender. She couldn't be packing much in the way of firepower in that space, secret weapon or no secret weapon."

"Have you mentioned this aspect to the commodore, sir?"

"Would it change anything, Ben?"

"Nooo. I suppose not."

"Then we'll let him carry on without any more cause for jumpiness than the presence of a vice admiral on board is already providing."

8

Crouched in his fitted acceleration cradle aboard the Djann vessel, the One-Who-Commands studied the motion of the charged molecules in the sensory tank before him.

"Now the death-watcher dispatches his messengers," he communed with the three link brothers who formed the Chosen Crew. "Now is the hour of the testing of Djann."

"Profound is the rhythm of our epic," the One-Who-Records sang out. "We are the chosen-to-be-heroic, and in our tiny cargo, Djann lives still, his future glory inherent in the convoluted spores!"

"It was a grave risk to put the destiny of Djann at hazard in this wild gamble," the One-Who-Refutes reminded his link brothers. "If we fail, the generations yet unborn will slumber on in darkness or perish in ice or fire."

"Yet if we succeed—if the New Thing we have learned serves well its function—then will Djann live anew!"

"Now the death messengers of the water beings approach," the One-Who-Commands pointed out. "Link well, brothers!

The energy aggregate waits for our directing impulse! Now we burn away the dross of illusion from the hypotheses of the theorists in the harsh crucible of reality!"

"In such a fire, the flame of Djann coruscates in unparalleled glory!" the One-Who-Records exulted. "Time has ordained this conjunction to try the timbre of our souls!"

"Then channel your trained faculties, brothers." The One-Who-Commands gathered his forces, feeling out delicately to the ravening nexus of latent energy contained in the thought shell poised at the center of the stressed-space field enclosing the fleeting vessel. "Hold the sacred fire, sucked from the living bodies of a million of our fellows," he exhorted. "Shape it, and hurl it in well-directed bolts at the death-bringers, for the future and glory of Djann!"

9

At noon, Carnaby and Sickle rested on a nearly horizontal slope of rock that curved to meet the vertical wall that swelled up and away overhead. Their faces and clothes were gray with the impalpable dust whipped up by the brisk wind. Terry spat grit from his mouth, passed a can of hot stew and a plastic water flask to Carnaby.

"Getting cool already," he said. "Must not be more'n ten above freezing."

"We might get a little more snow before morning." Carnaby eyed the milky sky. "You'd better head back now, Terry. No point in you getting caught in a storm."

"I'm in for the play," the boy said shortly. "Say, Lieutenant, you got another transmitter up there at the beacon station you might could get through on?"

Carnaby shook his head. "Just the beacon tube, the lens generators, and a power pack. It's a stripped-down installation. There's a code receiver, but it's only designed to receive classified instruction input."

"Too bad." They ate in silence for a few minutes, looking

out over the plain below. "Lieutenant, when this is over," Sickle said suddenly, "we got to do something. There's got to be some way to remind the Navy about you being here!"

Carnaby tossed the empty can aside and stood. "I put a couple of messages on the air, sub-light, years ago," he said. "That's all I can do."

"Heck, Lieutenant, it takes six years, sub-light, just to make the relay station on Goy! Then if somebody happens to pick up the call and boost it, in another ten years some Navy brass might even see it. And then if he's in a good mood, he might tell somebody to look into it, next time they're out this way."

"Best I could do, Terry, now that the liners don't call any more."

Carnaby finished his stew, dropped the can, watched it roll off downslope, clatter over the edge, a tiny sound lost in the whine and shrill of the wind. He looked up at the rampart ahead.

"We better get moving," he said. "We've got a long climb to make before dark."

10

Signal Lieutenant Pryor awoke to the strident buzz of his bunkside telephone.

"Sir, the commodore's called a Condition Yellow," the message deck NCO informed him. "It looks like that bandit blasted through our intercept and took out two Epsilon-classes while he was at it. I got a standby from command deck, and—"

"I'll be right up," Pryor said quickly.

Five minutes later, he stood with the on-duty signals crew, reading out an incoming from Fleet. He whistled.

"Brother, they've got something new!" he looked at Captain Aaron. "Did you check out the vector they had to make to reach their new position in the time they've had?"

"Probably a foulup in Tracking." Aaron looked ruffled, routed out of a sound sleep.

"The commodore's counting off the scale," the NCO said. "He figured he had 'em boxed."

The annunciator beeped. The yeoman announced *Malthusa's* commander.

"All right, you men," Broadly's voice had a rough edge to it now. "The enemy has an idea he can maul Fleet units and go his way unmolested. I intend to disabuse him of that notion! I'm ordering a course change. I'll maintain contact with this bandit until such time as units designated for the purpose have reported his neutralization! This vessel is under a Condition Yellow at this time, and I need not remind you that relevant sections of the manual will be adhered to with full rigor!"

Pryor and Aaron looked at each other, eyebrows raised. "He must mean business, if he's willing to risk straining seams with a full-vector course change," the former said.

"So we pull six on and six off until he gets it out of his system," Aaron growled. "I knew this cruise wasn't going to work out, as soon as I heard Old Carbuncle would be aboard."

"What's *he* got to do with it? Broadly's running this action."

"Don't worry, he'll be in it before we're through."

11

On the upper slope, three thousand feet above the plain, Carnaby and Terry hugged the rockface, working their way upward. Aside from the steepness of the incline, the going was of no more than ordinary difficulty here; the porous rock, resistant though it was to the erosive forces that had long ago stripped away the volcanic cone of which the remaining mass had formed the core, had deteriorated in its surface sufficiently to afford easy hand- and footholds. Now Terry paused, leaning against the rock. Carnaby saw that under the layer of dust, the boy's face was pale and drawn.

"Not much farther, Terry," he said. He settled himself in a secure position, his feet wedged in a cleft. His own arms were feeling the strain now; there was the beginning of a slight tremor in his knees after the hours of climbing.

"I didn't figure to slow you down, Lieutenant." Terry's voice showed the strain of his fatigue.

"You've been leading me a tough chase, Terry," Carnaby grinned across at him. "I'm glad of a rest." He noted the dark hollows under the lad's eyes, the pallor of his cheeks.

Sickle's tongue came out and touched his lips. "Lieutenant —you made a try—a good try. Turn back now. It's going to snow. You can't make it to the top in a blizzard."

Carnaby shook his head. "It's too late in the day to start down; you'd be caught on the slope. We'll take it easy up to the Roost; in the morning you'll have an easy climb down."

"Sure, Lieutenant. Don't worry about me." Terry drew a breath, shivering in the bitter wind that plucked at his snow jacket.

12

"What do you mean, lost him!" the bull roar of the commodore rattled the screen. "Are you telling me that this ragtag refugee has the capability to drop off the screens of the best-equipped tracking deck in the Fleet?"

"Sir," the stubborn-faced tracking officer repeated, "I can only report that my screens register nothing within the conic of search. If he's there—"

"He's there, Mister!" the commodore's eyes glared from under a bushy overhang of brows. "Find that bandit or face a court, Captain. I haven't diverted a ship of the Fleet Line from her course for the purpose of becoming the object of an Effectiveness Inquiry!"

The tracking officer turned away from the screen as it went white, met the quizzical gaze of the visiting signal lieutenant.

"The old devil's bit off too big a bite this time," he growled. "Let him call a court; he wouldn't have the gall."

"If we lose the bogie now, he won't look good back on

Vandy," Pryor said. "This is serious business, diverting from Cruise Plan to chase rumors. I wonder if he really had a positive ID on this track."

"Hell, no! There's no way to make a Positive at this range, under these conditions! After three years without any action for the newstapes, the brass are grabbing at straws."

"Well, if I were you, Gordie, I'd find that track, even it it turns out to be a tramp with a load of bootleg *dran.*"

"Don't worry. If he's inside the conic, I'll find him . . ."

13

"I guess . . . it's dropped twenty degrees . . . in the last hour," Terry Sickle's voice was almost lost in the shriek of the wind that buffeted the two men as they inched their way up the last yards toward the hut on the narrow rockshelf called Halliday's Roost.

"Never saw snow falling at this temperature before," Carnaby brushed at the ice caked around his eyes. Through the swirl of crystals as fine as sand, he discerned the sagging outline of the shelter above.

Ten minutes later, inside the crude lean-to built of rock slabs, he set to work chinking the gaping holes in the five-foot walls with packed snow. Behind him, Terry lay huddled against the back wall, breathing hoarsely.

"Guess . . . I'm not in as good shape . . . as I thought I was," he said.

"You'll be OK, Terry," Carnaby closed the gap through which the worst of the icy draft was keening, then opened a can of stew for the boy. The fragrance of the hot meat and vegetables made his jaws ache.

"Lieutenant, how you going to climb in this snow?" Sickle's voice shook to the chattering of his teeth. "In good weather, you might could have made it. Like this, you haven't got a chance!"

"Maybe it'll be blown clear by morning," Carnaby said

mildly. He opened a can for himself. Terry ate slowly, shivering uncontrollably. Carnaby watched him worriedly.

"Lieutenant," the boy said, "even if that call you picked up was meant for you—even if this ship they're after is headed out this way—what difference will it make one way or another if one beacon's on the air or not?"

"Probably none," Carnaby said. "But if there's one chance in a thousand he breaks this way—well, that's what I'm here for."

"But what's a beacon going to do, except give him something to steer by?"

Carnaby smiled. "It's not that kind of beacon, Terry. My station's part of a system—a big system—that covers the surface of a sphere of space a hundred lights in diameter. When there's an alert, each station locks in with the others that flank it, and sets up what's called a stressed field. There's a lot of things you can do with this field. You can detect a drive, monitor communications—"

"What if these other stations you're talking about aren't working?" Terry cut in.

"Then my station's not going to do much good," Carnaby said.

"If the other stations are still on the air, why haven't any of them picked up your TX's and answered?"

Carnaby shook his head. "We don't use the beacon field to chatter back and forth, Terry. This is a Top Security system. Nobody knows about it except the top command levels—and of course, the men manning the beacons."

"Maybe that's how they came to forget about you—somebody lost a piece of paper and nobody else knew!"

"I shouldn't be telling you about it," Carnaby said with a smile. "But I guess you'll keep it under your hat."

"You can count on me, Lieutenant," Terry said solemnly.

"I know I can, Terry," Carnaby said.

14

The clangor of the General Quarters alarm shattered the tense silence of the chart deck like a bomb through a plate glass window. The navigation officer whirled abruptly from the grametric over which he had been bending, collided with the deck chief. Both men leaped for the Master Position monitor, caught just a glimpse of a vivid scarlet trace lancing toward the emerald point targeted at the center of the plate before the apparatus exploded from its mounting, mowed the two men down in a hail of shattered plastic fragments. Smoke boiled, black and pungent, from the gutted cavity. The duty NCO, bleeding from a dozen gashes, stumbled toward the two men, turned away in horror, reached an emergency voice phone. Before he could key it, the deck under him canted sharply. He screamed, clutched at a table for support, saw it tilt, come crashing down on top of him . . .

On the message deck, Lieutenant Pryor clung to an operator's stool, listening, through the stridency of the alarm bell, to the frantic voice from command deck:

"All sections, all sections, combat stations! We're under attack! My God, we've taken a hit forward—"

The voice cut off, to be replaced by the crisp tones of Colonel Lancer, first battle officer:

"As you were! Sections G-987 and 989 damage control crews report! Forward armaments, safety interlocks off, stand by for firing orders! Message center, flash a code six to Fleet and TF Command. Power section, all selectors to gate, rig for full emergency power . . ."

Pryor hauled himself hand-over-hand to the main message console; the body of the code yeoman hung slackly in the seat harness, blood dripping from the fingertips of his dangling hand. Pryor freed him, took his place. He keyed the code six alarm into the pulse-relay tanks, triggered an emergency override signal, beamed the message outward toward the distant Fleet headquarters.

On the command deck, Commodore Broadly clutched a sprained wrist to his chest, stood, teeth bared, feet braced apart, staring into the forward imagescreen at the dwindling point of light that was the Djann blockade runner.

"The effrontery of the damned scoundrel!" he roared. "Lancer, launch another covey of U-95's! You've got over five hundred megaton/seconds of firepower, man! Use it!"

"He's out of range, Commodore," Lancer said coolly. "He booby-trapped us very neatly."

"It's your job to see that we don't blunder into traps, by God, Colonel!" He rounded on the battle officer. "You'll stop that pirate or I'll rip those eagles off your shoulders myself!"

Lancer's mouth was a hard line; his eyes were ice chips.

"You can relieve me, Commodore," his voice grated. "Until you do, I'm battle commander aboard this vessel."

"By God, you're relieved, sir!" Broadly yelled. He whirled on the startled exec standing by. "Confine this officer to his quarters! Order full emergency acceleration! This vessel's on Condition Red at Full Combat Alert until we overtake and destroy that sneaking snake in the grass!"

"Commodore—at full emergency without warning, there'll be men injured, even killed—"

"Carry out my commands, Captain, or I'll find someone who will!" the commodore's bellow cut off the exec. "I'll show that filthy, sneaking pack of spiders what it means to challenge a Terran fighting ship!"

On the power deck, Chief Powerman Joe Arena wiped the cut on his forehead, stared at the bloody rag, hurled it aside with a curse.

"All right, you one-legged deck apes!" he roared. "You heard it! We're going after the bandit, full gate—and if we melt our linings down to slag, I'll have every man of you sign a statement of charges that'll take your grandchildren two hundred years to pay off!"

15

In the near-darkness of the Place of Observation aboard the Djann vessel, the ocular complex of the One-Who-Commands glowed with a dim red sheen as he studied the apparently black surface of the sensitive plate. "The death watcher has eaten our energy weapon," he communicated to his three link brothers. "Now our dooms are in the palps of the fate spinner."

"The death watcher of the water beings might have passed us by," the One-Who-Anticipates signaled. "It was an act of rashness to hurl the weapon at it."

"It will make a mighty song," the One-Who-Records thrummed his resonator plates, tried a melancholy bass chord.

"But what egg-carrier will exude the brood-nourishing honeys of strength and sagacity in response to these powerful rhymes, if the stimulus to their creation leads us to quick extinction?" the One-Who-Refutes queried.

"In their own brief existence, these harmonies find their justification," the One-Who-Records attested.

"The death watcher shakes himself," the One-Who-Commands stated. "Now he turns in pursuit."

The One-Who-Records emitted a booming tone. "Gone are the great suns of Djann," he sang. "Lost are the fair worlds that knew their youth. But the spark of their existence glows still!"

"Now we fall outward, toward the Great Awesomeness," the One-Who-Anticipates commented. "Only the blackness will know your song."

"Draw in your energies from that-which-is-extraneous," the One-Who-Commands ordered. "Focus the full poignancy of your intellects on the urgency of our need for haste. All else is vain, now. Neither singer nor song will survive the vengeance of the death watcher if he outstrips our swift flight!"

"Though Djann and water being perish, my poem is eternal," the One-Who-Records emitted a stirring assonance. "Fly,

Djanni! Pursue, death watcher! Let the suns observe how we comport ourselves in this hour!"

"Exhort the remote nebulosities to attend our plight, if you must," the One-Who-Refutes commented. "But link your energies to ours or all is lost."

Silent now, the Djann privateer fled outward toward the Rim.

16

Carnaby awoke, lay in darkness listening to the wheezing of Terry Sickle's breath. The boy didn't sound good. Carnaby sat up, suppressing a grunt at the stiffness of his limbs. The icy air seemed stale. He moved to the entry, lifted the polyon flap. A cascade of powdery snow poured in. Beyond the opening a faint glow filtered down through banked snow.

He turned back to Terry as the latter coughed deeply, again and again.

"Looks like the snow's quit," Carnaby said. "It's drifted pretty bad, but there's no wind now. How are you feeling, Terry?"

"Not so good, Lieutenant," Sickle said weakly. He breathed heavily, in and out. "I don't know what's got into me. Feel hot and cold at the same time."

Carnaby stripped off his glove, put his hand on Sickle's forehead. It was scalding hot.

"You just rest easy here for a while, Terry. There's a couple more cans of stew, and plenty of water. I'll make it up to the top as quickly as I can. Soon as I get back, we'll go down together. With luck, I'll have you to Doc Link's house by dark."

"I guess . . . I guess I should have done like Doc said," Terry's voice was a thin whisper.

"What do you mean?"

"I been taking these hyposprays. Two a day. He said I better not miss one, but heck, I been feeling real good lately—"

"What kind of shots, Terry?" Carnaby's voice was tight.

"I don't know. Heck, Lieutenant, I'm no invalid! Or . . ." his voice trailed off.

"You should have told me, Terry."

"Gosh, Lieutenant—don't worry about me! I didn't mean nothing! Hell, I feel . . ." he broke off to cough deeply, rackingly.

"I'll get you back, Terry—but I've got to go up first," Carnaby said. "You understand that, don't you?"

Terry nodded. "A man's got to do his job, Lieutenant. I'll be waiting . . . for you . . . when you get back."

"Listen to me carefully, Terry." Carnaby's voice was low. "If I'm not back by this time tomorrow, you'll have to make it back down by yourself. You understand? Don't wait for me."

"Sure, Lieutenant, I'll just rest awhile. Then I'll be OK."

"Sooner I get started the sooner I'll be back." Carnaby took a can from the pack, opened it, handed it to Terry. The boy shook his head.

"You eat it, Lieutenant. You need your strength. I don't feel like I . . . could eat anything anyway."

"Terry, I don't want to have to pry your mouth open and pour it in."

"All right . . . but open one for yourself too . . ."

"All right, Terry."

Sickle's hand trembled as he spooned the stew to his mouth. He ate half of the contents of the can, then leaned back against the wall, closed his eyes. "That's all . . . I want . . ."

"All right, Terry. You get some rest now. I'll be back before you know it." Carnaby crawled out through the opening, pushed his way up through loosely drifted snow. The cold struck his face like a spiked club. He turned the suit control up another notch, noticing as he did that the left side seemed to be cooler than the right.

The near-vertical rise of the final crown of the peak thrust up from the drift, dazzling white in the morning sun. Carnaby examined the rockface for twenty feet on either side of the

hut, picked a spot where a deep crack angled upward, started
the last leg of the climb.

17

On the message deck, Lieutenant Pryor frowned into the
screen from which the saturnine features of Captain Aaron
gazed back sourly.

"The commodore's going to be unhappy about this," Pryor
said. "If you're sure your extrapolation is accurate—"

"It's as good as the data I got from Plotting," Aaron snapped.
"The bogie's over the make-or-break line; we'll never catch
him now. You know your trans-Einsteinian physics as well as
I do."

"I never heard of the Djann having anything capable of
that kind of acceleration," Pryor protested.

"You have now." Aaron switched off and keyed command
deck, passed his report to the exec, then sat back with a re-
signed expression to await the reaction.

Less than a minute later, Commodore Broadly's irate face
snapped onto the screen.

"You're the originator of this report?" he growled.

"I did the extrapolation," Aaron stared back at his commanding officer.

"You're relieved for incompetence," Broadly said in a tone
as harsh as a handsaw.

"Yessir," Aaron said. His face was pale, but he returned the
commodore's stare. "But my input data and comps are a matter of record. I'll stand by them."

Broadly's face darkened. "Are you telling me these spiders
can spit in our faces and skip off, scot-free?"

"All I'm saying, sir, is that the present acceleration ratios
will keep the target ahead of us, no matter what we do."

Broadly's face twitched. "This vessel is at full emergency
gain," he growled. "No Djann has ever outrun a Fleet unit in
a straightaway run."

"This one is . . . sir."

The commodore's eyes bored into Aaron's. "Remain on duty until further notice," he said, and switched off. Aaron smiled crookedly and buzzed the message deck.

"He backed down," he said to Pryor. "We've got a worried commodore on board."

"I don't understand it myself," Pryor said. "How the hell is that can outgaining us?"

"He's not," Aaron said complacently. "From a standing start, we'd overhaul him in short order. But he got the jump on us by a couple of minutes, after he lobbed the fish into us. If we'd been able to close the gap in the first half hour or so, we'd have had him; but at trans-L velocities, you get some strange effects. One of them is that our vectors become asymptotic. We're closing on him—but we'll never overtake him."

Pryor whistled. "Broadly could be busted for this fiasco."

"Uh-huh," Aaron grinned. "Could be—unless the bandit stops off somewhere for a quick one . . ."

After Aaron rang off, Pryor turned to study the position repeater screen. On it *Malthusa* was represented by a bright point at the center, the fleeing Djann craft by a red dot above.

"Charlie," Pryor called the NCOIC. "That garbled TX we picked up last watch; where did you R and D it?"

"Right about here, Lieutenant," the NCO flicked a switch and turned knobs; a green dot appeared near the upper edge of the screen.

"Hey," he said. "It looks like maybe our bandit's headed out his way."

"You picked him up on Y band; have you tried to raise him again?"

"Yeah, but nothing doing, Lieutenant. It was just a fluke—"

"Get a Y beam on him, Charlie. Focus it down to a cat's whisker and work a pattern over a one-degree radius centered around his MPP until you get an echo."

"If you say so, sir—but—"

"I do say so, Charlie! Find that transmitter, and the drinks are on me!"

18

Flat against the windswept rockface, Carnaby clung with his fingertips to a tenuous hold, feeling with one booted toe for a purchase higher up. A flake of stone broke away, and for a moment he hung by the fingers of his right hand, his feet dangling over emptiness; then, swinging his right leg far out, he hooked a knob with his knee, caught at a rocky rib with his free hand, pulled himself up to a more secure rest. He clung, his cheek against the iron-cold stone; out across the vast expanse of featureless grayish-tan plain, the gleaming whipped-cream shape of the next core rose ten miles to the south. A wonderful view up here—of nothing. Funny to think it could be his last. He was out of condition. It had been too long since his last climb.

But that wasn't the way to think. He had a job to do—the first in twenty-one years. For a moment, ghostly recollections rose up before him: the trim Academy lawns, the spit-and-polish of inspection, the crisp feel of the new uniform, the glitter of the silver comet as Anne had pinned it on . . .

That was no good either. What counted was here: the station up above. One more push, and he'd be there. He rested for another half minute, then pulled himself up and forward, onto the relatively mild slope of the final approach to the crest. Fifty yards above, the dull-gleaming plastron-coated dome of the beacon station squatted against the exposed rock, looking no different than it had five years earlier.

Ten minutes later he was at the door, flicking the combination latch dial with cold-numbed fingers. Tumblers clicked, and the panel slid aside. The heating system, automatically reacting to his entrance, started up with a busy hum to bring the interior temperature up to comfort level. He pulled off his gauntlets, ran his hands over his face, rasping the stubble there. There was coffee in the side table, he remembered. Fumblingly, with stiff fingers, he got out the dispenser, twisted the control cap, poured out a steaming mug, gulped it down. It was hot and bitter. The grateful warmth of it made him think of Terry, waiting down below in the chill of the half-ruined hut.

"No time to waste," be muttered to himself. He stamped up and down the room, swinging his arms to warm himself, then seated himself at the console, flicked keys with a trained ease rendered only slightly rusty by the years of disuse. He referred to an index, found the input instructions for code gamma eight, set up the boards, flipped in the pulse lever. Under his feet, he felt the faint vibration as the power pack buried in the rock stored its output for ten microseconds, fired it in a single millisecond burst, stored and pulsed again. Dim instrument lights winked on, indicating normal readings all across the board.

Carnaby glanced at the wall clock. He had been here ten minutes now. It would take another quarter hour to comply with the manual's instructions—but to hell with that gobbledegook. He'd put the beacon on the air; this time the Navy would have to settle for that. It would be pushing it to get back to the boy and pack him down to the village by nightfall as it was. Poor kid; he'd wanted to help so badly . . .

19

"That's correct, sir," Pryor said crisply. "I haven't picked up any comeback on my pulse, but I'll definitely identify the echo as coming from a JN type installation."

Commodore Broadly nodded curtly. "However, inasmuch as your instruments indicate that this station is not linked in with a net capable of setting up a defensive field, it's of no use to us." The commodore looked at Pryor, waiting.

"I think perhaps there's a way, sir," Pryor said. "The Djann are known to have strong tribal feelings. They'd never pass up what they thought was an SOS from one of their own. Now, suppose we signal this JN station to switch over to the Djann frequencies and beam one of their own signal patterns at them. They just might stop to take a look . . ."

"By God," Broadly looked at the signal lieutenant, "if he doesn't, he's not human!"

"You like the idea, sir?" Pryor grinned.

"A little rough on the beacon station if they reach it before we do, eh, Lieutenant? I imagine our friends the Djann will be a trifle upset when they learn they've been duped."

"Oh . . ." Pryor looked blank. "I guess I hadn't thought of that, sir."

"Never mind," Broadly said briskly, "the loss of a minor installation such as this is a reasonable exchange for an armed vessel of the enemy."

"Well . . ."

"Lieutenant, if I had a few more officers aboard who employed their energies in something other than assembling statistics proving we're beaten, this cruise might have made a record for itself—" Broadly cut himself off, remembereing the degree of aloofness due very junior officers—even juniors who may have raked some very hot chestnuts out of the fire.

"Carry on, Lieutenant," he said. "If this works out, I think I can promise you a very favorable endorsement on your next ER."

As Pryor's pleased grin winked off the screen, the commodore flipped up the red line key, snapped a brusque request at the bored log room yeoman.

"This will make Old Carbuncle sing another tune," he remarked almost gaily to the exec, standing by with a harassed expression.

"Maybe you'd better go slow, Ned," the latter cautioned, gauging his senior's mood. "It might be as well to get a definite confirmation on this installation's capabilities before we go on record—"

Broadly turned abruptly to the screen as it chimed. "Admiral, as I reported, I've picked up one of our forward beacon towers," Broadly's hearty voice addressed the screen from which the grim visage of the task force commander eyed him. "I'm taking steps to complete the intercept; steps which are, if I may say so, rather ingenious—"

"It's my understanding the target is receding on an I curve, Broadly," the admiral said flatly. "I've been anticipating a code thirty-three from you."

"Break off action?" Broadly's jaw dropped. "Now, Tom—"

"It's a little irregular to use a capital ship of the line to chase a ten-thousand-ton yacht," the task force commander ignored the interruption. "I can understand your desire to break the monotony with a little activity; good exercise for the crew, too. But at the rate the signal is attenuating, it's apparent you've lost her." His voice hardened. "I'm beginning to wonder if you've forgotten that your assignment is the containment of enemy forces supposedly pinned down under tight quarantine!"

"This yacht, as you put it, Admiral, blew two of my detached units out of space!" Broadly came back hotly. "In addition, he planted a missile squarely in my fore lazaret—"

"I'm not concerned with the details of your operation at this moment, Commodore," the other bit off the words like bullets. "I'm more interested in maintaining the degree of surveillance over my assigned quadrant that Concordiat Security requires. Accordingly—"

"Just a minute, Tom, before you commit yourself." Broadly's florid face was pale around the ears. "Perhaps you failed to catch my first remark: I have a forward station directly in the enemy's line of retreat. The intercept is in the bag—unless you countermand me."

"You're talking nonsense. The target's well beyond the Inner Line—"

"He's not beyond the Outer Line!"

The admiral frowned. His tight, well-chiseled face was still youthful under the mask of authority. "The system was never extended into the region under discussion," he said harshly. "I suggest you recheck your instruments. In the interim, I want to see an advice of a course correction for station in the length of time it takes you to give the necessary orders to your navigation section."

Broadly drew a breath, hesitated. If Old Carbuncle was right —if that infernal signal lieutenant had made a mistake—but the boy seemed definite enough about it. He clamped his jaw. He'd risked his career on a wild throw; maybe he'd acted a little too fast, maybe he'd been a little too eager to grab a chance at some favorable notice, but the die was cast now. If he turned back empty-handed, the entire affair would go into the record as a major fiasco. But if this scheme worked out . . .

"Unless the admiral wishes to make that a direct order," he heard himself saying firmly, "I intend to hold my course and close with the enemy. It's my feeling that neither the Admiralty nor the general public will enjoy hearing of casualties inflicted by a supposedly neutralized enemy who was then permitted to go his way unhindered." He returned the other's stare, feeling a glow of pride at his own decisiveness, and a simultaneous sinking sensation at the enormity of the insubordination.

The vice admiral looked back at him through narrowed eyes. "I'll leave that decision to you, Commodore," he said tightly. "I think you're as aware as I of what's at stake here."

Broadly stiffened at what was almost an open threat.

"Instruct your signal officer to pass full information on this supposed station to me immediately," the senior concluded curtly, and disappeared from the screen.

Broadly turned away, feeling all eyes on him. "Tell Pryor to copy his report to G at once," he said in a harsh voice. His eyes strayed to the exec's. "And if this idea of his doesn't work out, God help him." *And all of us,* he added under his breath.

20

As Carnaby reached for the door to start the long climb down, a sharp *beep!* sounded from the panel behind him. He looked back, puzzled. The bleat repeated, urgent, commanding. He swung the pack down, went to the console, flipped down the REC key.

". . . 37 *Ace Trey,*" an excited voice came through loud and clear. "*I repeat, cut your beacon immediately! JN 37 Ace Trey, Cincsec One-two-oh to JN 37 Ace Trey. Shut down beacon soonest! This is an Operational Urgent! JN 37 Ace Trey, cut beacon and stand by for further operational Urgent instructions. . . .*"

21

On the Fleet Command Deck aboard the flagship, Vice Admiral Thomas Carnaby, otherwise known as Old Carbuncle, studied the sector triagram as his communications chief pointed out the positions of the flagship, *Malthusa,* the Djann refugee, and the reported JN beacon station.

"I've researched the call letters, sir," the gray-haired signal major said. "They're not shown on any listing as an active station. In fact, the entire series of which this station would be a part is coded null; never reported in commission."

"So someone appears to be playing pranks, is that your conclusion, Henry?"

The signal officer pulled at his lower lip. "No, sir, not that, precisely. I've done a full analytical on the recorded signal that young Pryor first intercepted. It's plainly directed to Cincsec in response to their alert; and the ID is confirmed. Now, as I say, this series was dropped from the register; but at one time, such a designation *was* assigned *en bloc* to a proposed link in the Out Line. However, the planned installations never came to fruitition due to changes in the strategic position."

The vice admiral frowned. "What changes were those?"

"The task force charged with the establishment of the link encountered heavy enemy pressure. In fact, the cruiser detailed to carry out the actual placement of the units was lost in action with all hands. Before the program could be reinitiated, a withdrawal from the sector was ordered. The new link was never completed, and the series was retired, unused."

"So?"

"So . . . just possibly, sir, one of those old stations *was* erected before *Redoubt* was lost—"

"What's that?" The admiral rounded on the startled officer. "Did you say . . . *Redoubt?*" his voice was a hiss between set teeth.

"Y . . . yessir!"

"*Redoubt* was lost with all hands before she planted her first station!"

"I know that's what we've always thought, Admiral—"

The admiral snatched the paper from the major's hand. "JN 37 Ace Trey," he read aloud. "Why the hell didn't you say so sooner?" He whirled to his chief of staff. "What's Broadly got in mind?" he snapped the question.

The startled officer began a description of the plan to decoy the Djann vessel into range of *Malthusa's* batteries.

"Decoy?" the vice admiral snarled. The exec took a step backward, shocked at the expression on his superior's face. The latter spun to face his battle officer, standing by on the bridge.

"General, rig out an Epsilon series interceptor and get my pressure gear into it! I want it on the line ready for launch in ten minutes! Assign your best torchman as co-pilot!"

"Yessir!" The general spoke quickly into a lapel mike. The admiral flicked a key beside the hot-line screen.

"Get Broadly," he said in a voice like doom impending.

22

In the Djann ship, the One-Who-Commands stirred and extended a contact to his crew members. "Tune keenly in the scarlet regions of the spectrum," he communicated. "And tell me whether the Spinners weave a new thread in the tapestry of our fates."

"I sensed it but now, and felt recognition stir within me!" the One-Who-Records thrummed a mighty euphony. "A Voice of the Djann, sore beset, telling of mortal need!"

"I detect a strangeness," the One-Who-Refutes indicated. "This is not the familiar voice of They-Who-Summon . . ."

"After the passage of ninety cycles, it is not surprising that new chords have been added to the Voice, and others withdrawn," the One-Who-Anticipates pointed out. "If the link cousins are in distress, our path is clear!"

"Shall I then bend our fate line to meet the new Voice?" the One-Who-Commands called for a weighing. "The pursuers press us closely."

"The Voice calls; will we pervert our saga by shunning it?"

"This is a snare of the water beings, calculated to abort our destinies!" the One-Who-Refutes warned. "Our vital energies are drained to the point of incipient coma by the Weapon-Which-Feeds-On-Life! If we turn aside now, we place ourselves in the jaws of the destroyer!"

"Though the Voice lies, the symmetry of our existence demands that we answer its appeal," the One-Who-Anticipates declared.

The One-Who-Records sounded a booming arpeggio, combining triumph and defeat. "Let the Djann flame burn brightest in its hour of extinction!"

"I accede," the One-Who-Commands announced. "Though only the Great Emptiness may celebrate our immolation."

23

"By God, they've fallen for it!" Commodore Broadly smacked his fist into his hand and beamed at the young signal lieutenant. He rocked back on his heels, studying the position chart the plot officer had set up for him on the message deck. "We'll make the intercept about here." His finger stabbed at a point a fractional light from the calculated position of the newfound OL station.

He broke off as an excited voice burst from the intercom screen.

"Commodore Broadly, sir! Urgent from Task—" the yeoman's face disappeared from the screen to be replaced by the fierce visage of the vice admiral.

"Broadly, sheer off and take up course for station, and then report yourself under arrest! Commodore Baskov will take command: I've countermanded your damned-fool orders to the OL station! I'm on my way out there now to see what I can salvage—and when I get back, I'm preferring charges against you that will put you on the beach for the rest of your miserable life!"

24

In the beacon station atop the height of ground known as Thunderhead, Carnaby waited before the silent screen. The modifications to the circuitry had taken half an hour; setting up the new code sequences, another fifteen minutes. Then another half hour had passed, while the converted beacon beamed out the alien signal.

He'd waited long enough. It had been twenty minutes now since the last curt order to stand by; and in the hut a thousand feet below, Terry had been waiting now for nearly five hours, every breath he drew a torture of strangulation. The order had been to put the signal on the air, attempt to delay the enemy ship. Either it had worked, or it hadn't. If Fleet had any more instructions for him, they'd have to damn well deliver them in person. He'd done what was required. Now he had to see to the boy. Carnaby rose, again donned the backpack. Outside, he squinted up at the sky, a dazzle of mist-gray. Maybe the snow squall was headed back this way. That would be bad luck; it would be close enough as it was.

A bright point of light caught his eye, winking from high above, almost at zenith. Carnaby felt his heart take a leap in his chest that almost choked off his breath. For a moment he stood, staring up at it; then he whirled back through the door.

". . . *termand previous instructions!*" A new voice was rasping from the speaker. "Terminate all transmission immediately! JN 37, shut down power and vacate station! Repeat, an armed enemy vessel is believed to be vectored in on your signal! This is, repeat, a hostile vessel! You are to cease transmission and abandon station immediately—"

Carnaby's hand slapped the big master lever. Lights died on the panel; underfoot, the minute vibration jelled into immobility. Sudden silence pressed in like a tangible force—a silence broken by a rising mutter from above.

"Like that, eh?" Carnaby said to himself through clenched teeth. "Abandon station, eh?" He took three steps to a wall locker, yanked the door open wide, took out a short, massive power rifle, still encased in its plastic protective cover. He stripped the oily sheath away, checked the charge indicator; it rested on FULL.

There were foot-square windows set on each side of the twenty-foot room. Carnaby went to one, by putting his face flat against the armorplast panel, was able to see the ship, now a flaring fireball dropping in along a wide approach curve. As it descended swiftly, the dark body of the vessel took shape above the glare of the drive. It was a small, blunt-ended ovoid of unfamiliar design, a metallic black in color, decorated fore and aft with the scarlet blazons of a Djann war vessel.

The ship was close now, maneuvering to a position directly

overhead. A small landing craft detached itself from the parked ship, plummeted downward like a stone, with a shrill whistling of high-speed rotors settled in across the expanse of broken rock in a cloud of pale dust. The black plastic bubble atop the landing sled split like a clam shell; a shape came into view, clambered over the cockpit rim and stood, a cylindrical bronze-black body, slung by leathery mesenteries from the paired U-frames that were its ambulatory members, two pairs of grasping limbs folded above.

A second Djann emerged, a third, a fourth. They stood together, immobile, silent, while a minute ticked past. Sweat trickled down the side of Carnaby's face. He breathed shallowly, rapidly, feeling the almost painful thudding of his heart.

One of the Djann moved suddenly, its strange, jointless limbs moving with twinkling grace and speed. It flowed across to a point from which it could look down across the plain, then angled to the left and reconnoitered the entire circumference of the mountaintop. Carnaby moved from window to window to watch it. It rejoined the other three; briefly, they seemed to confer. Then one of the creatures, whether the same one or another Carnaby wasn't sure, started across toward the hut.

Carnaby moved back to a position in the lee of a switch gear cabinet. A moment later the Djann appeared at the door. At a distance of fifteen feet, Carnaby saw the lean limbs, like leather-covered metal, the heavy body, the immense faceted eyes that caught the light and sent back fiery glints. For thirty seconds, the creature scanned the interior of the structure. Then it withdrew. Carnaby let out a long, shaky breath, watched it lope back to rejoin its companions. Again, the Djann conferred; then one turned to the landing craft . . .

For a long moment, Carnaby hesitated: he could stay where he was, do nothing, and the Djann would reboard their vessel and go their way; and in a few hours, a Fleet unit would heave into view off Longone, and he'd be home safe. But the orders had been to delay the enemy . . .

He centered the sights of the power gun on the alien's body, just behind the forelegs, and pushed the firing stud.

A shaft of purple fire blew the window from its frame, lanced out to smash the up-rearing alien against the side of the sled, send it skidding in a splatter of molten rock and metal. Carnaby swung the rifle, fired at a second Djann as the group scattered; the stricken creature went down, rolled, came up, stumbling on three limbs. He fired again, knocked the creature spinning, dark fluid spattering from a gaping wound in the barrel-like body. Carnaby swung to cover a third Djann, streaking for the plateau's edge; his shot sent a shower of molten slag arcing high from the spot where it disappeared.

He lowered the gun, stepped outside, ran to the corner of the building. The fourth Djann was crouched in the open, thirty feet away; Carnaby saw the glitter of a weapon gripped in the hand-like members springing from its back. He brought the gun up, fired in the same instant that light etched the rocks, and a hammer-blow struck him crushingly in the side, knocked him back against the wall. He tasted dust in his mouth, was aware of a high, humming sound that seemed to blank out his hearing, his vision, his thoughts . . .

He came to, lying on his side against the wall. Forty feet away, the Djann sprawled, its stiff limbs out-thrust at awkward angles. Carnaby looked down at his side. The Djann particle gun had torn a gaping rent in his suit, through which he could see bright crimson beads of frozen blood. He groped, found the rifle, dragged it to him. He shook his head to clear away the mist that seemed to obscure his vision. At every move, a terrible pain stabbed outward from his chest. *Ribs broken,* he thought. *Something smashed inside, too.* It was hard for him to breathe. The cold stone on which he lay seemed to suck the heat from his body.

Across the hundred-foot stretch of frost-shattered rock, a soot-black scar marked the spot where the escaping Djann had gone over the edge. Painfully, Carnaby propped the weapon to cover the direction from which attack might come. Then he slumped, his face against the icy rock, watching down the length of the rifle barrel for the next move from the enemy.

25

"Another four hours to shift, Admiral," General Drew, the battle commander acting as co-pilot aboard the racing interceptor said. "That's if we don't blow our linings before then."

"Bandit still holding position?" The admiral's voice was a grate as of metal against metal.

Drew spoke into his lip mike, frowned at the reply. "Yes, sir, *Malthusa* says he's still stationary. Whether his locus is identical with the LN beacon's fix or not, he isn't sure at that range."

"He could be standing by off-planet, looking over the ground," the admiral muttered half to himself.

"Not likely, Admiral. He knows we're on his tail."

"I know it's not likely, damn it!" the admiral snarled. "But if he isn't, we haven't got a chance . . ."

"I suppose the Djann conception of honor requires these beggars to demolish the beacon and hunt down the station personnel, even if it means letting us overhaul them," Drew said. "A piece of damn foolishness on their part, but fortunate for us."

"Fortunate, General? I take it you mean for yourself and me, not the poor devil that's down there alone with them."

"Just the one man? Well, we'll get off more cheaply than I imagined then." The general glanced sideways at the admiral, intent over the controls. "After all, he's Navy. This is his job, what he signed on for."

"Kick that converter again, General," Admiral Carnaby said between his teeth. "Right now you can earn your pay by squeezing another quarterlight out of this bucket."

26

Crouched in a shallow crevice below the rim of the mesa where the house of the water beings stood, the One-Who-Records quivered under the appalling impact of the death emanations of his link brothers.

"Now it lies with you alone," the fading thought came from the One-Who-Commands. "But the water being, too, is alone, and in this . . . there is . . . a certain euphony . . ." The last fragile tendril of communication faded.

The One-Who-Records expelled a gust of the planet's noxious atmosphere from his ventral orifice-array, with an effort freed his intellect of the shattering extinction-resonances it had absorbed. Cautiously, he probed outward, sensing the strange, fiery mind-glow of the alien . . .

Ah, he too was injured! The One-Who-Records shifted his weight from his scalded forelimb, constricted further the flow of vital fluids through the damaged section of his epidermal system. He was weakened by the searing blast that had scored his flank, but still capable of action; and up above, the wounded water being waited.

Deftly, the Djann extracted the hand weapon from the sheath strapped to his side, holding it in a two-handed grip, its broad base resting on his dorsal ridge, its ring lenses aligned along his body. He wished briefly that he had spent more *li* periods in the gestalt tanks, impressing the weapon's use syndromes on his reflex system; but feckless regrets made poor scansion. Now indeed the display podium of existence narrowed down to a single confrontation: a brief and final act in a century-old drama, with the fate of the mighty epic of the Djann resting thereon. The One-Who-Records sounded a single, trumpet-like resonance of exultation, and moved forward to fulfill his destiny.

27

At the faint bleat of sound, Carnaby raised his head. How long had he lain here, waiting for the alien to make its move? Maybe an hour, maybe longer. He had passed out at least twice, possibly for no more than a second or two; but it could have been longer. The Djann might even have gotten past him—or crawled along below the ridge, ready now to jump him from a new angle . . .

He thought of Terry Sickle, waiting for him, counting on him. Poor kid. Time was running out for him. The sun was dropping low, and the shadows would be closing in. It would be icy cold inside the hut and down there in the dark the boy was slowly strangling, maybe calling for him . . .

He couldn't wait any longer. To hell with the alien. He'd held him long enough. Painfully, using the wall as a support, Carnaby got to his hands and knees. His side felt as though it had been opened and packed with red-hot stones—or were they ice-cold? His hands and feet were numb. His face ached. Frostbite. He'd look fine with a frozen ear. Funny, how vanity survived as long as life itself . . .

He got to his feet, leaned against the building, worked on breathing. The sky swam past him, fading and brightening. His feet felt like blocks of wood; that wasn't good. He had a long way to go. But the activity would warm him, get the blood to flowing, except where the hot stones were. He would be lighter if he could leave them here. His hands moved at his side, groping over torn polyon, the sharp ends of broken wires . . .

He brought his mind back to clarity with an effort. Wouldn't do to start wandering now. The gun caught his eye, lying at his feet. Better pick it up; but to hell with it, too much trouble. Navy property. But can't leave it here for the enemy to find. Enemy. Funny dream about a walking oxy tank, and—

He was looking at the dead Djann, lying awkward, impossible, thirty feet away. No dream. The damn things were real. He was here, alone, on top of Thunderhead—

But he couldn't be. Flitter was broken down. Have to get another message off via the next tramp steamer that made planetfall. Hadn't been one for . . . how long . . . ?

Something moved, a hundred feet away, among the tumble of broken rock. Carnaby ducked, came up with the blast rifle, fired in a half-crouch from the hip, saw a big dark shape scramble up and over the edge, saw the wink of yellow light, fired again, cursing the weakness that made the gun buck and yaw in his hands, the darkness that closed over his vision. With hands that were stiff, clumsy, he fired a third time at the swift-darting shape that charged toward him; and then he was falling, falling . . .

28

Stunned by the direct hit from the energy weapon of the water being, the One-Who-Records fought his way upward through a universe shot through with whirling shapes of fire, to emerge on a plateau of mortal agony.

He tried to move, was shocked into paralysis by the cacophony of conflicting motor- and sense-impressions from shattered limbs and organs.

Then I, too, die, the thought came to him with utter finality. *And with me dies the once-mighty song of Djann . . .*

Failing, his mind groped outward, calling in vain for the familiar touch of his link brothers—and abruptly, a sharp sensation impinged on his sensitivity complex. Concepts of strange and alien shape drifted into his mind, beating at him with compelling urgency; concepts from a foreign brain:

Youth, aspirations, the ring of the bugle's call to arms. A white palace rearing up into yellow sunlight; a bright banner, rippling against blue sky, and the shadows of great trees ranked on green lawns. The taste of grapes, and an odor of flowers; night, and the moon reflected from still water; the touch of a

*soft hand and the face of a woman, invested with a supernal
beauty; chords of a remote music that spoke of the inexpres-
sibly desirable, the irretrievably lost . . .*

"Have we warred then, water beings?" the One-Who-Records sent his thought outward. "We who might have been
brothers . . . ?" With a mighty effort, he summoned his wan-
ing strength, sounded a final chord in tribute to that which
had been, and was no more.

29

Carnaby opened his eyes and looked at the dead Djann
lying in the crumpled posture of its final agony against the wall
of the hut, not six feet from him. For a moment, a curious sensation of loss plucked at his mind.

"Sorry, fellow," he muttered aloud. "I guess you were doing
what you had to do, too."

He stood, felt the ground sway under his feet. His head
was light, hot; a sharp, clear humming sounded in his ears.
He took a step, caught himself as his knees tried to buckle.

"Damn it, no time to fall out now," he grunted. He moved
past the alien body, paused by the door to the shed. A waft
of warm air caressed his cold-numbed face.

"Could go inside," he muttered. "Wait there. Ship along in
a few hours, maybe. Pick me up . . ." He shook his head
angrily. "Job's not done yet," he said clearly, addressing the
white gleam of the ten-mile-distant peak known as Cream Top.
"Just a little longer, Terry," he added. "I'm coming."

Painfully, Carnaby made his way to the edge of the plateau,
and started down.

30

"We'd better make shift to sub-L now, Admiral," Drew said,
strain showing in his voice. "We're cutting it fine as it is."

"Every extra minute at full gain saves a couple of hours," the vice admiral came back.

"That won't help us if we kick out inside the Delta limit and blow ourselves into free ions," the general said coolly.

"You've made your point, General!" The admiral kept his eyes fixed on his instruments. Half a minute ticked past. Then he nodded curtly.

"All right, kick us out," he snapped, "and we'll see where we stand."

The hundred-ton interceptor shuddered as the distorters whined down the scale, allowing the stressed-space field that had enclosed the vessel to collapse. A star swam suddenly into the visible spectrum, blazing at planetary distance off the starboard bow at three o'clock high.

"Our target's the second body, there." He pointed. The copilot nodded and punched the course into the panel.

"What would you say, another hour?" the admiral bit off the words.

"Make it two," the other replied shortly. He glanced up, caught the admiral's eye on him.

"Kidding ourselves won't change anything," he said steadily.

Admiral Carnaby narrowed his eyes, opened his mouth to speak, then clamped his jaw shut.

"I guess I've been a little snappy with you, George," he said. "I'll ask your pardon. That's my brother down there."

"Your . . . ?" the general's features tightened. "I guess I said some stupid things myself, Tom," he frowned at the instruments, busied himself adjusting course for an MIT approach to the planet.

31

Carnaby half jumped, half fell the last few yards to the narrow ledge called Halliday's Roost, landed awkwardly in a churn of powdered wind-driven snow. For a moment, he lay sprawled, then gathered himself, made it to his feet, tottered to the hollow concealing the drifted entrance to the hut. He lowered himself, crawled down into the dark, clammy interior.

"Terry," he called hoarsely. A wheezing breath answered him. He felt his way to the boy's side, groped over him. He lay on his side, his legs curled against his chest.

"Terry!" Carnaby pulled the lad to a sitting position, felt him stir feebly. "Terry, I'm back! We have to go now, Terry . . ."

"I knew . . ." the boy stopped to draw an agonizing breath, "you'd come . . ." He groped, found Carnaby's hand.

Carnaby fought the dizziness that threatened to close in on him. He was cold—colder than he had ever been. The climbing hadn't warmed him. The side wasn't bothering him much now; he could hardly feel it. But he couldn't feel his hands and feet, either. They were like stumps, good for nothing. . . . Clumsily, he backed through the entry, bodily hauling Terry with him.

Outside, the wind lashed at him like frozen whips. Carnaby raised Terry to his feet. The boy leaned against him, slid down, crumpled to the ground.

"Terry, you've got to try," Carnaby gasped out. His breath seemed to freeze in his throat. "No time . . . to waste . . . got to get you to . . . Doc Link . . ."

"Lieutenant . . . I . . . can't . . ."

"Terry . . . you've got to try!" He lifted the boy to his feet.

"I'm . . . scared . . . Lieutenant . . ." Terry stood swaying, his slight body quivering, his knees loose.

"Don't worry, Terry." Carnaby guided the boy to the point from which they would start the climb down. "Not far, now."

"Lieutenant . . ." Sickle caught at Carnaby's arm. "You . . . better . . . leave . . . me." His breath sighed in his throat.

"I'll go first," Carnaby heard his own voice as from a great distance. "Take . . . it easy. I'll be right there . . . to help . . ."

He forced a breath of sub-zero air into his lungs. The bitter wind moaned around the shattered rock. The dusky afternoon sun shed a reddish light without heat on the long slope below.

"It's late," he mouthed the words with stiff lips. "It's late . . ."

32

Two hundred thousand feet above the surface of the outpost world Longone, the Fleet interceptor split the stratosphere, its receptors fine-tuned to the Djann energy-cell emission spectrum.

"Three hundred million square miles of desert," Admiral Carnaby said. "Except for a couple of deserted townsites, not a sign that any life ever existed here."

"We'll find it, Tom," Drew said. "If they'd lifted, *Malthusa* would have known—hold it!" He looked up quickly, "I'm getting something—yes! It's the typical Djann idler output!"

"How far from us?"

"Quite a distance . . . now it's fading . . ."

The admiral put the ship into a screaming deceleration curve that crushed both men brutally against the restraint of their shock frames.

"Find that signal, George," the vice admiral grated. "Find it and steer me to it, if you have to pick it out of the air with psi!"

"I've got it!" Drew barked. "Steer right, on 030. I'd range it at about two thousand kilometers. . . ."

33

On the bald face of an outcropping of wind-scored stone, Carnaby clung one-handed to a scanty hold, supporting Terry with the other arm. The wind shrieked, buffeting at him; sand-fine snow whirled into his face, slashing at his eyes, already half-blinded by the glare. The boy slumped against him, barely conscious.

His mind seemed as sluggish now as his half-frozen limbs.

Somewhere below there was a ledge, with shelter from the wind. How far? Ten feet? Fifty?

It didn't matter. He had to reach it. He couldn't hold on here, in this wind; in another minute he'd be done for.

Carnaby pulled Terry closer, got a better grip with a hand that seemed no more a part of him than the rock against which they clung. He shifted his purchase with his right foot—and felt it slip. He was falling, grabbing frantically with one hand at the rock, then dropping through open air—

The impact against drifted snow drove the air from his lungs. Darkness shot through with red fire threatened to close in on him; he fought to draw a breath, struggling in the claustrophobia of suffocation. Loose snow fell away under him, and he was sliding. With a desperate lunge, he caught a ridge of hard ice, pulled himself back from the brink, then groped, found Terry, lying on his back under the vertically rising wall of rock. The boy stirred.

"So . . . tired . . ." he whispered. His body arched as he struggled to draw breath.

Carnaby pulled himself to a position beside the boy, propped himself with his back against the rock. Dimly, through ice-rimmed eyes, he could see the evening lights of the settlement, far below; so far . . .

He put his arm around the thin body, settled the lad's head gently in his lap, leaned over him to shelter him from the whirling snow. "It's all right, Terry," he said. "You can rest now."

34

Supported on three narrow pencils of beamed force, the Fleet interceptor slowly circuited the Djann yacht, hovering on its idling null-G generators a thousand feet above the towering white mountain.

"Nothing alive there," the co-pilot said. "Not a whisper on the life-detection scale."

"Take her down." Vice Admiral Carnaby squinted through S-R lenses which had darkened almost to opacity in response to the frost-white glare from below. "The shack looks all right, but that doesn't look like a Mark 7 Flitter parked beside it."

The heavy Fleet boat descended swiftly under the expert guidance of the battle officer. At fifty feet, it leveled off, orbited the station.

"I count four dead Djann," the admiral said in a brittle voice.

"Tracks," the general pointed. "Leading off there . . ."

"Put her down, George!" The hundred-foot boat settled in with a crunching of rock and ice, its shark's prow overhanging the edge of the tiny plateau. The hatch cycled open; the two men emerged.

At the spot where Carnaby had lain in wait for the last of the aliens, they paused, staring silently at the glossy patch of dark blood, and at the dead Djann beside it. Then they followed the irregularly spaced footprints across to the edge.

"He was still on his feet—but that's about all," the battle officer said.

"George, can you operate that Spider boat?" The admiral indicated the Djann landing sled.

"Certainly."

"Let's go."

35

It was twilight half an hour later when the admiral, peering through the obscuring haze of blown snow, saw the snow-drifted shapes huddled in the shadow of an overhang. Fifty feet lower, the general settled the sled in to a precarious landing on a narrow shelf. It was a ten-minute climb back to their objective.

Vice Admiral Carnaby pulled himself up the last yard, looked across the icy ledge at the figure in the faded blue polyon cold suit. He saw the weathered and lined face, glazed with ice; the closed eyes, the gnarled and bloody hands, the great wound in the side.

The general came up beside him, stared silently, then went forward.

"I'm sorry, Admiral," he said a moment later. "He's dead. Frozen. Both of them."

The admiral came up, knelt at Carnaby's side.

"I'm sorry, Jimmy," he said. "Sorry . . ."

"I don't understand," the general said. "He could have stayed up above, in the station. He'd have been all right there. What in the world was he doing down here?"

"What he always did," Admiral Carnaby said. "His duty."